GHOST TOWN

NATE STACK

OTHER TITLES BY NATE STACK

Chiara X
Silver Age Series Book 1 (2017)

Lady Vampyr
Silver Age Series Book 3 (2019)

Book design by *design for a small planet*
Cover photo by Lario Tus, used under license from Shutterstock

ISBN 10: 1985875764
ISBN 13: 978-1985875760
Library of Congress Control Number: 2018958997

EDB Media Publishing
New York, New York

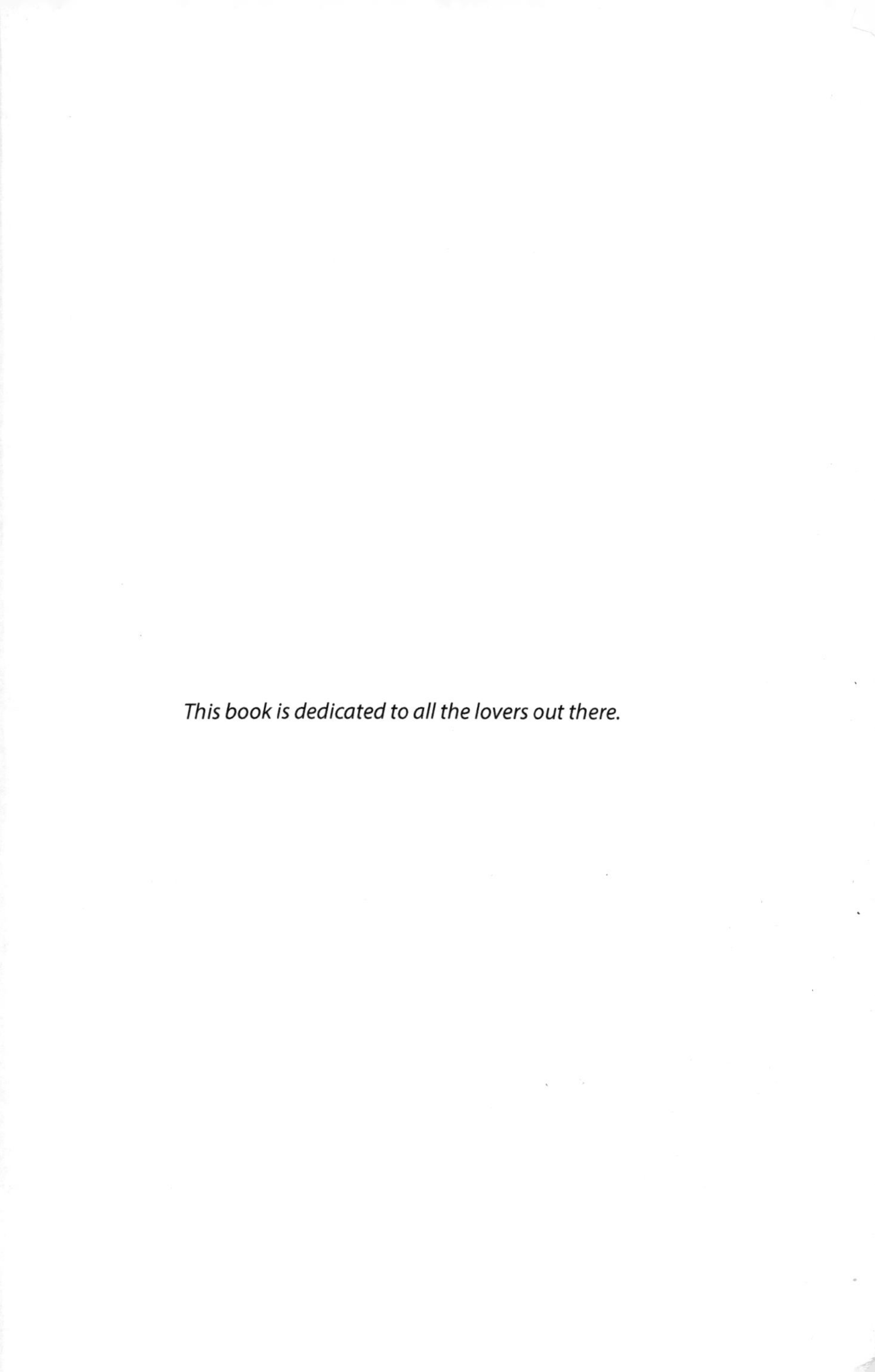

This book is dedicated to all the lovers out there.

NATE STACK

GHOST TOWN

CHAPTER ONE

"Ah...excuse me...Miss?" said the tall, lean, ruggedly handsome man in his midtwenties holding a six-gun in his hand. "Are you lost?"

He was speaking to a woman who was about five feet seven inches tall and around twenty-five years of age with pale skin, dark eyes, and long, straight black hair that fell over her shoulders and down to the middle of her back. She said nothing, looking confused.

"You're naked, Miss," said the tall man. "Do you know where you put your clothes?"

The young woman looked down at her body and then around at her surroundings, the prairie spreading out in front of her and stretching for miles in all directions to the mountains that bordered on every side. Still she said nothing.

"My name is Wyatt Earp, Miss," said the man. "I'm the sheriff in these parts, and I'm just trying to figure who you are and how you got here."

"Here?" the young woman asked. "Where is here?"

"You're in Ghost Town," said Sheriff Earp. "Out by the abandoned train station that closed 'cause the railroad never came through."

"Ghost Town?" she asked, bewildered. "I have no idea how I got here."

A rifle clicked behind her. The young woman turned around slowly and faced two people on horseback. One was a very young girl, barely a teen, and the other was a man who could have been in his forties. Both pointed their guns at her as she stood in front of them.

"Have I done something wrong?" she asked.

"Reckon we're here to find out," said Earp, taking off his jacket and placing it around the young woman's shoulders. "Better put this on."

"Thank you," she said. "I'm not sure what I'm doing here."

"Bill," the sheriff asked, "does this naked woman look familiar to you?"

"Nope," said the older man, a wrangler named Rhino Bill Cody. "Never seen her before in my life."

Sitting atop a large brown horse with white spots that covered its hindquarters, Rhino Bill wore buckskin pants, a fur vest with no sleeves, and a wide-brimmed, high-crowned wrangler's hat known as the "boss of the plains."

The girl who rode with him had long, soft-brown curls, kewpie-doll lips, and a slender frame encased in buckskin overalls, a flannel shirt, and a beaver-fur coat. In her hands she held a long-range rifle.

"What year is this?" the young woman asked.

"It's 1865, Miss," said the sheriff.

"1865?" she said, puzzled. "You're kidding me, right?"

"As a sworn officer of the law," said the sheriff, "I always tell the truth."

"Who are you, Miss?" asked the young girl.

"My name is Nikki," the young woman replied. "Nikki Hale...and I think I'm a ghost from the future."

They all laughed.

"Sounds a might confusing," said Rhino Bill.

"Well," said Nikki, "how do you think I feel?"

"My name is Bill," he said. "How come you're naked?"

"Ghosts don't wear clothes, Bill," said Nikki. "Slows us down."

"You look..." Earp blushed. "I mean, very alive to me."

"My name is Annie," said the girl on the horse, "Annie Oakley."

"Hello, Annie," said Nikki. "It's a pleasure to meet you."

"And I'm Sheriff Earp," the sheriff repeated, extending his hand. "Wyatt."

"A pleasure, Wyatt," Nikki said. She smiled into his twinkling eyes.

"Do I know you?" he asked, lifting his hat off his head and scratching his whiskered chin. "You seem so…familiar."

"You…" she said.

"We'd better get moving," said Annie. "It'll be getting dark soon."

Rhino Bill lifted his shotgun. "This time, I'll be ready for them."

"Annie's right," said Earp. "No one stays out after dark in Ghost Town."

"I don't really have anywhere to go," said Nikki. "I'm lost."

"Why don't you stay at the sheriff's house?" Annie said. "He's got plenty of room."

"I'm sure my place is not fit for a lady," said Earp, holding his hat in hand. Suddenly Nikki trembled, seized with the chills.

"Are you all right?" asked the sheriff.

Nikki looked across the field to where two men dressed in miner's overalls stood. They wore metal hats and held lamps in their hands.

"What is it, Nikki?" asked Earp.

"Those men?" she asked. "Who are they?"

"Men? What men?"

"There," she said, pointing. "Don't you see them? Those two men standing in the road, staring at us?"

"'Fraid, not," Earp said. "The sun out here plays tricks sometimes. Even I've been fooled by things I've seen."

When Nikki looked again, the men were gone.

"It's getting dark," said Annie. "We'd best be heading back."

"You're welcome to stay with me," said Earp, quietly. "I mean…you know, until we figure out what to do with you."

"I accept your offer, Sheriff," she said. "And thanks. I'd like to find some real clothes to wear, if that's possible."

"Oh," Earp said sheepishly. "Annie can help you with that."

"We can head there now, if you want," said Annie, offering her hand. "Climb aboard."

"That would be great." Nikki grabbed Annie's hand and pulled herself up onto the back of her horse.

"I'll follow," said Earp as he walked away to retrieve his horse.

Annie turned her horse around and headed out past the dilapidated train station toward the center of town. Rhino Bill followed.

"You OK back there?" Annie asked her passenger.

"Annie," said Nikki, "I have to ask. Why is everyone so afraid of the dark?"

There were no people on Main Street except for a mortician hitching up his hearse in front of the boarded-up saloon. The stores were mostly all closed—what remained were a jail, a saloon, a brothel, a hotel, a funeral parlor, a church and small graveyard, a general store, a blacksmith's forge, stables, and an opium den. Farther out of town, where the remaining residential homes still stood against the elements, lived people who had managed to survive by putting up passing rhino wranglers needing a place to stay and providing supplies for their journey west to the coast.

Down the dusty street on the back of her palomino rode Annie, with Nikki behind her as the sun set in the west, the town becoming dark momentarily until the evening torches were lit.

"Are you sure I'll be able to find clothes around here?" asked Nikki. "This town looks deserted and spooky."

"You'll see," said Annie. "It's right over here."

"Where? It's too dark to see anything."

Annie stopped her horse in front of a boarded-up millinery shop next to the boarded-up saloon and slid off her horse, her rifle still in her hand. Nikki jumped down after her, and Annie tied the horse to the porch post.

"This is Miss Windi's dress shop," said Annie, pointing it out.

Nikki looked at the boarded-up storefront and said, "Oh…it looks like it's closed."

"Nope," Annie said. "It's open."

Rhino Bill emerged from the darkness behind them and stopped in front of the boarded-up saloon. He dismounted and looked nervously in all directions while pointing his shotgun at the darkness.

"Bill," said Annie, "relax, will ya? You're making Nikki nervous."

"I…" Nikki began but faltered.

"No worries, Miss," said Rhino Bill. "Everything is under control."

"I asked Annie why everyone seems to be afraid of the dark," said Nikki. "She didn't answer."

"Smart girl," he said. "I'm headed next door to the saloon, so you'll know where to find me if anything unpleasant shows up."

Rhino Bill tied up his horse in front of the saloon.

"What did you mean by 'unpleasant'?" asked Nikki.

Ignoring her, he knocked twice, and the board-covered door opened. He stepped inside and disappeared as the door closed behind him.

"Nikki," said Annie. "Over here."

The door to the boarded-up millinery was open, the interior lit by kerosene lanterns that hung from the ceiling. Annie beckoned Nikki to come in.

"How did you do that?" Nikki said.

"Yup," Annie said. "Miss Windi is very special."

"Special? In what way?"

"She can do magical things."

"Like what?"

"She can blow up a dust storm on a calm day and spin gale-force winds to knock down trees," said Annie. "If she wants to."

"It's a wonder she has any time to run a dress shop," said Nikki, half joking.

Nikki followed Annie into the shop, noticing immediately that the walls and floors were covered with cobwebs, dust, and even dead critters. On the grimy shelves sat folded bolts of fabric, all of them in tatters, damaged by rodents. On the walls, faded satin paper had turned brown with age and flaked off in spots from front to back. Behind the sales counter near the back of the shop, two female mannequins bookended the entrance to the dressing room. The kerosene lamps cast strange shadows, making it seem that someone was dancing on the walls and ceiling.

"Windi's almost here," Annie said.

"Look," said Nikki. "I may be from the future, but I wasn't born yesterday. What are you talking about?"

"Windi is here."

As Annie spoke the words, a great gust of wind blew through the shop, clearing the dust, dirt, and dead things out through the front door and blowing the velvet cover off a large, freestanding, six-foot-tall mirror, exposing its smoky glass.

Nikki stepped forward but tripped on the fallen cover resting on the floor, hitting her forehead on the glass and falling backward to the floor.

"Nikki!" Annie shouted.

Nikki sat up, feeling dazed and confused. The contents of the shop spun around her like a whirlwind, and the amazing thing was the shop looked more organized than before, pristine and rugged at the same time.

Nikki got up off the floor and walked slowly around the newly organized store. Linen and laces, so perfect for the dry desert heat, had replaced the cobwebs and dust piles. Hats formerly unrecognizable under layers of dust now shone in the warm light from the kerosene lamps. She turned back and saw Annie standing near the tall mirror, her rawhide overalls replaced by a simple cotton dress. Lace ribbons tied back her curly hair.

"You look amazing," Nikki said incredulously. "But what just happened here?"

"Windi," Annie replied.

Nikki turned and looked around.

"No, over here," said another female voice in the room softly.

Looking back, Nikki saw a woman standing in front of the smoky mirror. She cast no reflection.

"My name is Windi Langtrees," said the woman. She was in her late twenties and had cream-colored skin and long, wavy flaxen hair. She wore a fashionable dress of the day that featured a bustle in the back and a peekaboo cutout in front that offered glimpses of her leg and lace pantaloons.

"Hi, I'm Nikki Hale," Nikki said, extending her hand, "and I think I'm losing my mind."

"How so?" Windi asked.

"Uh...you, for instance. A few minutes ago, this shop was a disaster, and now it's completely organized. How do you explain that?"

Windi stepped away from the mirror and up close to Nikki, who stared back at her, aware Windi was evaluating her in some capacity.

"May I remove this?" asked Windi. She slowly removed Sheriff Earp's jacket from Nikki's shoulders and let it drop to the floor.

"I obviously need some new clothes," said Nikki.

"I have already taken your measurements," said Windi. "A finished garment can be picked up on the counter to your left."

"That fast?" said Nikki.

"That fast," said Windi.

"Annie," said Nikki, "could you please tell me what's going on?"

"Windi is special."

"I can see that."

"Try it on, Nikki," Annie said, squealing in anticipation. "It's so pretty."

Nikki picked up the dress and quickly donned it, turning back to stare at her reflection in the mirror. The dress was a simple white linen frock that tied at the waist and barely covered the knee.

"You look beautiful," said Annie. "Like a bride."

Nikki looked into the mirror and did not recognize the person looking back. She'd somehow changed from a teenager into a young woman in her midtwenties who was a foot taller, more muscular, and exotically striking with dark hair and eyes.

"I agree the dress looks great on me," said Nikki, "but it's not really appropriate, I think, for Ghost Town. Maybe you have something more rustic?"

"You don't like it?" Windi asked, deeply serious.

"She's right," said Annie. "Them pretty dresses get beat up real fast."

"I do like the dress," said Nikki, "but maybe I could try on a fur vest like the one Rhino Bill wears. And a pair of denim slacks; a crisp, long-sleeved white linen shirt; and low-heeled boots might be better suited to the terrain."

Nikki turned to thank Windi, but she had already gone, this time without casting so much as a gentle breeze.

"I don't think she liked me much," said Nikki.

"Shucks, she's fine," said Annie. "Look what she brought ya."

On the floor at Nikki's feet were the vest, denim slacks, linen shirt, and boots she'd requested, along with a man's hat similar to the one worn by Sheriff Earp, only smaller. She quickly removed the dress and put on the new clothes.

"Oh...what about payment?" Nikki asked.

"No charge."

"But Annie, these clothes are handmade," Nikki said. "I'd like to pay Windi something."

"You got any money?"

"Well...no," Nikki said. "I arrived naked and without—"

"It's getting late," said Annie, ominously. "We'd best get you over to Sheriff Earp's place."

"I suppose it's a waste of time to ask you again what's going on in this town," said Nikki.

"It's what creeps around at night that's got folks so scared," Annie said, mysteriously. "The dead and the undead...and the creatures who only come out after dark."

CHAPTER TWO

The boarded-up saloon next to the boarded-up millinery was open to those who took refuge from the dark night. One by one, the townsfolk wandered in from the street—gunslingers, ranch hands, runaways, criminals, lawmen, older women, politicians, ladies of the evening, and the town banker all entered Lillie Langtrees's saloon to forget their troubles and have a good time. The dim light cast by hanging kerosene lamps and candle-lit chandeliers concealed the saloon's filth—along with the sawdust lining the floor lay a snoozing stray dog, a fallen drunk, and the occasional dead chicken.

Most of the saloon's patrons were seated around the large circular bar, which filled most of the room. Behind it was a circular stage where a woman dressed in a one-piece swimsuit was dancing, moving her arms in unison with the piano music emanating from the corner, where a large woman sat at the instrument and played.

"Where's Lillie?" demanded the drunken town banker, who proceeded to spill his drink all over the bar.

"Hey!" shouted the man standing next to him. "Be careful, sir."

"A pox on you, my good man," the banker said.

"Settle down," warned the rough-looking bartender, "or else you'll get thrown out."

"Where the freck is Lillie?" the banker whined, and he reached for another drink.

The bartender used a short wooden club to smash the banker's wrist. "You're cut off."

"I want Lillie," cried the banker, too drunk to feel pain, and then with a smile, he fell and landed face down on the floor.

"Throw that drunk out," ordered Miss Lillie Langtrees. The famous singer and actress from the continent of Atlantica, where she headlined supper clubs and high-end bars, had appeared next to the piano player.

The light from a nearby kerosene lantern spotlighted her face. Only about five feet four inches tall, Lillie wore a red-sequined off-the-shoulder gown with a rear bustle that reached to the sawdusty floor, her upswept hair held in place by a feather comb.

She moved around the room, pushing alcohol and working up the crowd in expectation of the evening's entertainment. At Miss Lillie's establishment, along with a floor show, her clientele was offered the chance to meet one of the young, sexy multiracial dancers for a night—women who had been brought to town from other continents through Lillie's business interests.

"We want the women!" a few drunks shouted in unison. "Let um dance for us."

"You want my dancers?" asked Miss Lillie as she climbed to the stage in her tight dress with help from the burly bartender. "Thank you, dear. You can step down now."

The woman dancing in the swimsuit left the stage.

"So, you want to see my dancers?" asked Lillie. "I used to be a dancer. Now I just sit around and count my money."

Miss Lillie dropped the straps from her creamy white shoulders to reveal the tops of her very large breasts. The alcohol-powered men sitting around the bar went wild, clapping, whistling, and trying to stand on their seats.

Onstage, Miss Lillie removed the rest of her top, covering her naked breasts with her bare arms. "I'd like to introduce you to my sisters," she said. "They'll take over from here. Windi, Terra, Oceanna, and Ginger—the Gilded Lilies!"

The four women, each clothed in a single bright color, ran out from a side door from behind the bar, leaped up on the stage, and began dancing to piano music that was seriously off key, kicking their legs up in the air and revealing their undergarments, which drove the crowd of rowdy drunks wild.

Seated at the circular bar but seeming oblivious to the entertainment was Rhino Bill. He drank whiskey from a shot glass.

Sheriff Wyatt Earp walked up behind him and took a seat.

"Need some company, Bill?" asked Sheriff Earp.

"Always," said Rhino Bill after taking a swig. "That's why I married my little Annie—so she'd outlive me and I wouldn't have to die alone."

"She's taken Nikki to my ranch," said Earp. "But I can't shake the feeling that I've met her somewhere before."

"It's been a while since your wife's death," said Rhino Bill. "Maybe she reminds you of Katie."

"No, it's something she said. Time travel. It struck a chord."

"Something strange is going on," said Rhino Bill. "Bar-keep—four more whiskeys."

"If I could move through time," said Sheriff Earp, "back and forth within seconds, think about how many crimes I could prevent."

"I'd rather be right here," said Rhino Bill. "In my own time."

The bartender placed the four drinks in from of them, and both men reached for a glass and swallowed the whiskey shots one after the other until all four glasses were empty.

"What are you boys talking about over here?" asked Miss Lillie. "Secrets will get you killed in Ghost Town…or have you forgotten, Sheriff?"

"We're not sharing secrets, Miss Lillie, I assure you," said Sheriff Earp. "No, we were talking about something that happened today out by the old railroad station."

"You mean the naked girl who showed up without any recollection of where she'd come from?" asked Lillie.

"You know about that?"

"There's nothing in town I don't know about, Sheriff," she said, "including the size of your—"

At that very moment, a group of six dancers wearing almost-see-through fishnet costumes burst out of the back room and threw fist-sized pom-poms at the drunken crowd, who were on their feet, clapping along with the piano music that kept the dancers twirling.

"More drinks here for my old friends," said Lillie to her bartender.

"No, seriously—how did you find out?" Sheriff Earp asked, his tone solemn.

"Nikki—is what she's called?" said Lillie. "She was in my sister Windi's store earlier, and she told me all about her."

"You have a lot of sisters, Miss Langtrees," said Rhino Bill. "I count at least five."

"Four," she said. "I'm the original."

The original Lillie was an elemental who had the power to give birth to four very special sisters. Her sister Windi could conjure hurricane-force winds and cyclone-style rains—even whip up lethal tornadoes—to get her way. Their third sister, a redhead named Ginger, had the ability to control fire. The fourth, possessing the power to rival fire, was Oceanna, and she could divert large amounts of water from lakes, rivers, and oceans and turn it into destructive weapons. The youngest sister—and perhaps the most powerful—was Terra, an earth elemental who controlled the movement of the ground.

The bartender placed multiple drinks in front of Rhino Bill and Sheriff Earp.

"Have a drink, boys," said Lillie as she turned to leave. "I've got a saloon to run."

She moved on, and between the music, the drunken patrons, and the destruction from physical fighting, the saloon grew very noisy. To calm things down, Miss Lillie ordered the girls to get closer to their johns, so they gradually paired off with men and escorted them through a passageway into the brothel next door.

"Sheriff, what do you know about the supernatural?" asked Rhino Bill.

"You mean ghosts? Just what I read in books."

Two drunken rhino wranglers nearby started a fistfight over the attentions of the smallest dancer, Little Daisy.

"This here's *my* little pony," declared one of them.

At first they punched each other, but then they turned to her, each grabbing an arm, and they pulled her in opposite directions.

"Over my dead body!" said the wrangler, yanking again on Little Daisy's arm.

"Let go of me!" she screamed. "You're tearing me a—"

Before she could finish, the drunken rhino wranglers pulled so hard on her arms that they literally ripped them off her body. Little Daisy bled to death on the floor.

Someone screamed.

The piano player stopped playing.

The two wranglers just stood there, each holding one of Little Daisy's dangling, bleeding arms.

"Now, why did you boys have to do that?" the sheriff asked.

He got off his stool, picked up and quickly drank another shot of whiskey, and then turned to face the wranglers, who were standing on the other side of the circular bar.

Quickly dropping the body parts, they drew their guns, but they were too slow. Sheriff Earp had already pulled out his six-guns, and they dropped their weapons.

"Bill, I'll see you around," said the sheriff. "Got to lock up these dangerous drunks before they can do any more harm."

"Wait a second," said Lillie Langtrees indignantly. "Who is going to pay me for the girl?"

A focus on the bottom line had made Lillie Langtrees a very wealthy woman. She lived extravagantly in Ghost Town, enjoyed the finer things shipped in from back east, and lived above the saloon in a suite of lavishly decorated rooms.

That night after the saloon closed, Lillie went upstairs to her private bedroom at the back of the building. She opened the door slowly to make sure no one was inside and then strode in and began to undress. Draped in her favorite sheer nightgown, she sat at her vanity and combed her long chestnut-brown hair in front of the large oval mirror.

"I thought you'd never come back," said an unseen female from the dark side of the room.

"Patience, sister," said a third female voice from the same spot.

"Good. You're both here," said Lillie. "Was your trip north a success?"

Two attractive young women stepped into the light.

They looked exactly like Lillie except for their different coloring and clothes.

"Yes. We broke into the gunpowder depository at Fort Stump," said Ginger, who had changed her stage outfit and now wore jeans, a cotton shirt pulled tight at the waist, and rugged, worn boots.

"I created a river out of a little stream so we could transport it quickly back here by water," Oceanna said. "And Terra kept it covered with dirt so the gunpowder wouldn't explode."

"Your boyfriend should be happy," said Ginger. "We got exactly what he wanted."

"Excellent work, sisters," said Miss Lillie. "But he's not my boyfriend. He is my business partner."

"Whatever," said Ginger.

"Sister," said Oceanna, "be kind."

"Doc will be pleased," said Lillie. "He plans to sell half and use the other half to build his bomb."

"I don't really care what it's used for," said Ginger. "I just like stealing things."

"Be wary of this Doc Holliday," said Oceanna. "He might be using you and the rest of us to achieve his goals."

"Such as?" Lillie asked.

"What every man wants," Oceanna said, "to run his own show. And, he's certainly not taking us along for the ride."

"Well, Lillie," said Ginger, "I can see you're not listening. So I'm off."

With that, she burst into flames and flew out an open window, singeing the lace curtains as she passed through.

"You should think about what I told you, sister," said Oceanna. "That man is clouded by revenge. You can never really trust him."

"I love money," Lillie replied without hesitation, "so I don't really have much choice."

"Love can be misleading," said Oceanna as she adjusted her garter, "and the woman is the one who usually gets screwed."

"I didn't know you were a philosopher, sister dear," said Lillie. "Maybe next time keep it to yourself."

"It's time for me to depart as well," said Oceanna, and she turned from a solid, breathing object into a clear liquid and washed through the open window like a wave, flowing onto the roof and down the drainpipe into the street.

Lillie continued to brush her long, thick hair until she heard a scratching sound in a dark corner of her room. She stopped brushing and looked around but saw nothing suspicious.

"Doc?" she called out. "Is that you?"

Then she heard a giggle.

"What do you want?" she cried out.

The doorknob started to shake and then turn slowly back and forth, as if someone or something was trying to get inside. She got up and walked toward the door. There was a loud bang, and she jumped back, nearly falling over her footstool.

The doorknob rattled again, turned again for a few seconds, and then stopped.

"Lillie," a soft, barely audible voice called through the door. "Let me in."

"Go away!" she said in a panic. "I command you!"

"I need to…ahhhh…" the voice said, still barely above a whisper, "even the score."

"Leave me alone," said Lillie, frozen in place. "You're dead!"

Silence.

Then came the sound of heavy footsteps walking away.

Lillie walked cautiously toward her door, stood for a few seconds, and then reached for the doorknob. Slowly she opened the door and looked into the hallway. No one stood on the other side. The hallway was empty.

"Julian," she called over the stair rail.

A young man of about twenty, heavily built and wearing a bowler hat, came to the bottom of the stairs and looked up.

"Yes, ma'am?"

"Were you just up here walking around?" she asked.

"No, ma'am," he said. "Been down here the whole time."

"Did you see anyone lurking about near my room?"

"No, ma'am, I haven't."

Frustrated, Lillie returned to her room and slammed the door behind her.

"Must be losing it," she said, sitting back down in front of the mirror. She picked up her hairbrush and resumed brushing her hair. As she moved her candelabrum closer to the mirror to get a better look, she thought she noticed someone standing at the rear of the room. Lillie turned around quickly, but no one was there.

Turning back toward the mirror, she was confronted by the face of a heavyset young man with a neatly cropped beard staring back at her. She gasped.

"No!" Lillie screamed, covering her eyes. "I thought I was rid of you!"

The ghostly apparition floated out of the mirror and materialized into a short man wearing a tight suit.

"You stole from me, Lillie," said the ghost. "I will not rest until I have justice."

"Never going to happen," Lillie said. "I'm glad I killed you."

"Your lack of remorse is not surprising," said the ghost, "but someday, Lillie, you will pay for your crimes...and I'll be watching."

"Threats from a ghost," she said, laughing. "I'm not impressed."

At that moment, all the glass in her windows blew out into the street, the wooden walls shook, and her oval mirror cracked down the middle and broke into small pieces, some barely missing her face.

The ghost was gone.

Sheriff Wyatt Earp escorted the two drunken wranglers toward the town's jail at the end of an empty Main Street, but they had to make multiple stops to allow for vomiting and falling down. Earp finally managed to get them into the jailhouse without incident and placed the two wranglers into one of the empty cells.

"You need to sober up so I can arrest you for murder," said the sheriff as he closed the cell door. "Right now you're both too drunk to comprehend."

The rhino wranglers passed out on their cots, and Earp went to his desk. "You're so forgetful, darling," said a female voice from out of nowhere. "Your keys are in your breast pocket."

Earp reached into his breast pocket and pulled out the cell key.

"Thanks," he said aloud in response, but then he quickly realized no one was there.

The sheriff headed over to the cell and properly locked it, staring at the sleeping men in the cots for a few seconds.

"They killed me," said the female voice. "Why didn't you stop them?"

Sheriff Earp pulled his six-guns out of their holsters and spun around to face—no one, only silence and emptiness. Unnerved, Earp emerged from the jail area and checked all the doors and windows as well as the back porch, and no one was there.

Back inside, Earp took a seat at his desk, put his head down, and fell fast asleep.

He had a dream. In this dream, he was standing naked under the noonday sun on an empty Main Street in Ghost Town. At the other end of the street stood the woman he'd met earlier—Nikki. She reminded Earp of his dead wife, Katie, who had disappeared many years ago and was presumed dead.

The woman walked slowly toward him as he approached her.

People now stood on the wooden sidewalks on both sides of the street, staring at him and laughing at his nakedness. None of them were recognizable, and many wore animal masks and faded clothing from an earlier time when the town had been just an outpost, before the gold miners came and made the town rich. Then the people all raised their arms in unison and pointed.

"Guilty!" they said as one. "You did not protect her."

Earp stopped walking, confused.

"Guilty!"

The crowd surrounded Earp, with their bodies pressing against him and making him feel claustrophobic.

"Guilty!" the chorus screamed in unison.

The masked people now came out onto the street and walked toward him.

Suddenly Sheriff Earp found himself standing on a gallows with a knotted rope around his neck.

"As punishment, you must die," declared a man wearing a judge's robe and a mask of a rabbit's head. Then a female wearing a fox-head mask and robe ascended the gallows stairs. When she reached the top, she stopped and looked at him.

"Nikki?" he asked. "Is that you behind the mask?"

The female stepped closer.

"Do you have any last words before you're hanged?" asked the judge.

"I would like to see who is under that mask," said Earp.

"Very well," said the judge. "Come closer, my dear, and take off your mask."

The female approached Earp and lifted the mask off her head and slipped off her robe. It was not Nikki Hale under the fox mask. It was his dead wife, Katie. Her body was covered head to toe in large human bite marks that were infected and oozed pus.

"Why did you let them, Wyatt?" she asked. "I wanted to live and have our baby."

"You're not my wife!" he screamed. "This is a dream, and I'll wake up soon."

"I'm sorry to have to tell you this, Wyatt," she said, moving her rotting head in for a kiss. "Life is a dream, and death is the waking up."

The hangman pulled the lever, and the floor gave way beneath Sheriff Earp, who gagged and gasped and kicked his legs.

CHAPTER THREE

As they neared their destination, Annie Oakley held her gun tightly and kept her eye on everything going on around them while Nikki Hale, who was seated behind her, held tight to a kerosene lamp they'd picked up off a lamppost. Their journey from the dress shop to the sheriff's home did not end without incident. On a dark side street off Main Street, Nikki thought she heard a baby's cry.

"Annie," she said, "can we stop and check? It sounds like a baby's in trouble."

"Don't think so," said Annie. "Could be a trap."

"Couldn't we take just a quick look?" Nikki said.

"We could," Annie said, "and chances are we'd never be heard from again."

"Seriously?"

"Nikki," said Annie, "there's one thing you gotta understand—this town is dead, and a lot of its people are too. Inside."

"Including babies?"

"Yes."

"Including the sheriff?"

"Yup, in a way," Annie said. "Same as me."

Nikki agreed to move on without checking, and they arrived a bit later at Sheriff Earp's small ranch on a hill outside of town. Nikki dismounted and held the kerosene lamp while Annie dismounted, and they made their way to the front door of a small one-bedroom house built for Sheriff Earp and his wife, Katie.

"Go on in," said Annie as Nikki stood on the porch. "It's not locked."

"Feels strange to enter another person's home when they're out," said Nikki, opening the door and entering. They lit the kerosene lamps near the front door and surveyed the room. The house was neatly kept, and, from the looks of it, hardly ever used. It almost seemed as if the woman of the house were still there in some way—everything looked so feminine.

"How long has his wife been gone?" Nikki asked.

"Almost six years now," said Annie as she looked around. "I guess nothing has changed since then."

"It's pretty isolated here," said Nikki. "Very alone."

"The sheriff likes it that way," said Annie. "Says it's comforting."

Nikki walked through the living room and took in the nature paintings on the walls, the family daguerreotypes on the mantel depicting Katie and Wyatt as a young couple in love, and the doilies still in place on the backs of the chairs.

"I'll bet you're hungry," said Annie. "I've got some food in my pack—I'll be right back."

She turned and headed out the front door while Nikki continued to explore. She spied a small piano in a dark corner and playfully struck a few keys, but the piano was badly out of tune. As Nikki started to walk away, the piano began to play on its own. Turning back quickly, she found no one there.

"It's not much," said Annie as she entered the room.

"Did you hear that?" asked Nikki.

"What?"

"That piano," said Nikki. "It played by itself, not even five feet from where I stood."

"Like I said, Nikki—Ghost Town is a haunted place, and anything is possible."

"I'm starting to believe that," said Nikki. "The trick is to keep from going mad."

"You need to get yourself a good man," said Annie with a laugh, "like the one I got. Makes life a whole lot easier and safer, and it's nicer when you share."

"Thanks for the advice," Nikki said. "I'll stay single for now—at least until I figure out how I got here and how I can get back home."

"Well, I'm going to settle down for tonight," said Annie.

"You're leaving?"

"I'll be right outside the front door," she said. "Don't need to worry about me none."

"Why don't you sleep inside tonight, Annie?" asked Nikki. "It's dark out there, and there's plenty of room in here."

"Shucks, I haven't slept inside since I was a little baby," said Annie. "Too old to adjust now. Good night, Nikki."

"Good night, Annie. Thanks for everything."

Annie smiled at Nikki and left, shutting the door behind her.

Alone now, Nikki sat down and ate some of the food Annie had left on the table. Tired from the long day, she picked up her kerosene lamp and went into the bedroom.

Inside the room was a large, dark, ornately carved mahogany bed that stood in stark contrast to the simplicity of the pine floor and walls. A simple cotton nightgown with an embroidered lace collar was laid over the bed on the left side. She quickly shed her clothes, donned the nightgown, climbed under the covers, and fell fast asleep.

Ghost Town's schoolmarm slept late into the afternoon, as her classes were conducted exclusively at night. She needed to rest most of the day to prepare.

Her routine was always the same. A few minutes after sunset, she'd wake up and climb out of the big mahogany bed—a gift from her parents back east—throw on a floral robe, pull back her long dark hair, and tie it with ribbon before heading to the kitchen.

"Good afternoon, Sunshine," said Katie Earp to her husband, Sheriff Wyatt Earp, who sat at the breakfast table reading a book. "I am starved. What do we have to eat?"

"First a kiss," he said. "I made eggs when I heard you get up. They're over on the stove."

"You are the best husband in...town," said Katie, "and I'm the lucky one who married you."

Katie leaned over to kiss Earp on the lips, and they lingered. Then Katie went to the stove and picked up her plate, joined her husband at the table, and began to eat.

"There's no salt," said Earp. "I'll pick some up in town this evening."

"Thank you, dear husband," Katie said with a smile. "What would I do without you?"

"Perish, I imagine."

She finished eating and got up from the table.

"Even though I can't cook," she said, spinning around in the room, "I am a great dancer, among other things. Wouldn't you agree?"

"Yup."

"As a matter of fact," she said as she pulled Earp up out of his chair, "I think it's time we tried to make a baby."

"Right now?"

"Yup."

Earp dropped the book on the table, and followed Katie into the bedroom. She fell over the bed, and he sat on the end and started to pull off his boots and unbutton his shirt, trousers, and undergarments. He stood up naked before her, his body tall and lean, muscular without being bulky, and boasting a few scars, probably from bullet wounds he'd suffered during the Great War.

Katie stood up on the big bed and let her robe fall. Now naked, she jumped into his strong arms, and he caught her and lay her down on the bed. He placed himself on top of her, entering her and passionately thrusting as Katie groaned with pleasure as they made love. Earp had never before met a woman like Katie, one who enjoyed making love as much as he did. She was willing to try anything and often took the lead.

"Katie," said Earp, "I love you so much."

"I love you too, Wyatt," she said. "Only don't be so serious all the time, OK?"

She pushed him over and landed on top of him. He pushed up, and she pushed down, and it only made the coupling better.

"Oh!" she said, sitting up. "It's getting late! We'd better get going."

"But I'm not done yet," said Earp.

"The boys will be angry if I'm late," said Katie, "and then they won't settle down."

"OK," said Earp. "I'm getting up."

"I wish I didn't have to leave," said Katie, wistfully.

"You don't," said Earp. "They won't miss you, and I don't like your going out there so late at night alone."

But Katie was already out of bed and had started to dress.

"I'm not alone," she said. "You escort me there and wait outside, so I don't really have to worry."

"Unless I have to be somewhere as sheriff," said Earp. "Then you're on your own, Nikki."

"Nikki?" asked Katie. "Who is Nikki?"

"I'm not sure," Earp said. "I don't know anybody by that name. It just popped into my head."

"Not the perfect ending," said Katie on her way out of the bedroom.

"Sorry," he said like a sad puppy. "The lovemaking was great."

He dressed quickly and joined her in the living room.

"I'm serious about not wanting you to go out there," he said. "Those boys are not what they seem."

"What are you saying?" she asked.

"They don't go out in daylight," said Earp. "They only come out at night."

"You think those little boys are what?" she asked. "Monsters?"

"Nothing in this town would surprise me," he said.

"They have an allergy to sunlight," Katie said, "and they need me to teach them at night, that's all."

"If I didn't think you could take care of yourself," said Earp, "I wouldn't let you go."

"You're very superstitious, Wyatt. I'm not afraid."

"You're the naive one. Those boys you teach are not the victims—they're the predators."

"They're just hungry for knowledge."

"Yes, hungry for something," he said, skeptically.

Katie threw a knitted shawl over her shoulders, pulled on her leather boots, and headed toward the front door. Then she stopped suddenly and turned around.

"You resent the fact that I make my own money."

"Yes, dear," he mumbled, following her out the front door. "Your carriage awaits."

"You harnessed my horse?" she asked. She stepped up into her one-horse carriage and grabbed the reins.

"Earlier," he said.

She blew Sheriff Earp a kiss while he climbed up on his horse and turned its head in the direction of town.

"Look," he said, pulling up next to her carriage, "I'm concerned about you."

"I'll be careful, you worrywart," she said. "I promise."

He clucked to his horse, and she led the carriage out of the yard, following her husband as he headed toward Ghost Town on horseback. They soon reached a fork in the road just outside town, one path leading to Main Street and the other to the south side of town, with its fading estates of the gold-bust ex-rich. The boys Katie tutored lived there, residing in a rambling, decaying twelve-bedroom house that sat at the end of a dead-end street. Earp took the southern road, and they ended up in front of the all-but-abandoned mansion. Its single kerosene lantern, hung near the front door, illuminated the front porch and lit the walkway.

Earp sat on his horse and watched the house for movement. Katie stepped out of her carriage, tied up her horse, and walked slowly toward the front door.

"OK, I'll see you in the morning, Wyatt," she said, and then she turned back. "Don't forget to come back for me. I love you."

"I won't forget. I love you, too."

Katie blew him another kiss and mounted the steps to the front porch, where she picked up the lantern and knocked. The door slowly opened, and Katie entered the empty hallway, passing dusty, sheet-covered furniture, cobweb-filled rooms, and dark passageways until she arrived at the ancient kitchen. There, she opened the back door and looked out toward a small glass building in the backyard.

"Hello? It's Miss Katie. I've come back to teach."

Giggles.

The sound came from the greenhouse that was used as Katie's schoolroom.

"Don't be afraid," she said. "I'm here because you asked me to come."

More giggles.

"Please come out of hiding," she said. "So we can get started."

Silence.

Katie put her kerosene lantern down on the countertop and opened drawers until she found candles. She placed them in a dusty silver candelabrum that had been left on a table and used straw from the floor to capture the lamp's flame and light all four candles. The additional light in the dust-covered kitchen revealed that it hadn't been used in a very long time.

"I'm on my way out to join you," she called out. "I've brought you a new book tonight that we can all read together."

A weak, childlike voice answered from inside the greenhouse. "We're waiting."

Katie looked through the back door into the pitch-black, moonless night, picked up the candelabrum and the kerosene lantern off the counter, and exited the kitchen, stepping on the dewy grass that separated the mansion from the greenhouse. Katie moved quickly, balancing the lights she held, which cast strange shadows all over the backyard. As she reached the greenhouse door, the back door to the main house slammed shut behind her with a bang that cracked the window glass into a replica of a spider's web. Panicked, Katie kicked opened the glass door to the greenhouse and held the kerosene lantern out in front of her.

"Stop!" cried a small voice in the darkness. "Don't bring that light any closer. It hurts."

The double illumination of the lantern and candelabrum exposed five small boys ranging in age from three and a half to twelve years huddling tightly together in the back corner of the greenhouse. In the seconds it took for Katie to look away, she glimpsed their skin, as pale as snow and almost translucent. They had no hair on their heads and had rounded generic faces, droopy mouths, and beady, almost animal eyes. They were quite frightening.

"There you are," said Katie, placing the kerosene lamp on the floor and blowing out the candles. "I'm sorry if the light hurt you."

The boys all wore the same uniform: gray woolen jackets, white shirts, and gray woolen shorts. They were barefoot and didn't really walk; rather, they shuffled along using both their legs and arms to propel them forward. Only the light could stop them, and Katie had extinguished half of hers to build their trust.

"You can come out now," she said. "The bad light is gone."

The kerosene lantern was still lit and illuminated a circle on the floor that the boys were careful to step around as they presented themselves to Katie. She backed away a few steps, unfamiliar with their harsh looks, ravenous moods, and deadly intentions.

"Please don't hurt me," she said, and backed away toward the glass door.

"The lantern," the oldest boy said. "Give it to us."

Before she could reach the door handle, Katie tripped over something on the floor, hitting her head on the glass door with a thud. The impact didn't break the glass but opened a gash on Katie's head that spilled blood.

"No!" she shouted. "I need the lantern to see my way in the dark."

"Darkness is our friend," said a small voice. "We love the darkness."

Katie pulled out her handkerchief and swabbed her head, wiping away the blood. "Tonight," she said to distract them, "I brought you a book that tells the story of a boy who travels along a mighty river and discovers new and wonderful things."

"Tell us!" they demanded, settling down on the floor in front of her. "Tell us about the boy."

"First I have to move the lantern," she said, pulling a book out of her handbag, "so that I will have light to read you this wonderful book."

Growls.

Some of the boys got restless and agitated at the smell of Katie's blood.

"Before I begin," she said, "I'd like to ask about your parents. I'd like to meet them, if I may."

Feral growls.

"Our parents are not here," said the second youngest, who seemed to possess the largest vocabulary. "They've gone."

"Gone?" she asked. "But who is taking care of you?"

"We take care of ourselves," they replied in unison. "We are Brood."

That same evening, Sheriff Wyatt Earp rode into Ghost Town and headed for the jailhouse. The jail, a detached single-story brick building with barred windows, a steel door, and gas lighting, sat at the north end of town, close to the mortuary.

Main Street was empty as Earp pulled his horse close to the jailhouse window and looked inside. There sat his sworn-in night deputy, Rhino Bill Cody, asleep in his chair, his feet up on the desk. The sheriff dismounted, slowly opened the door, and entered the small jail. He approached his sleeping deputy and kicked the chair.

"What the..." Rhino Bill exclaimed, jumping up. "Sheriff, you scared me half to death!"

"You're supposed to be guarding the prisoners, Bill," said Earp. "Not taking a nap."

"Ain't got no prisoners, Sheriff," said Rhino Bill. "It's been a quiet night."

Earp walked back to the cells.

"I thought you said we had no prisoners," said Earp. "Who's this?"

"Oh, him," said Rhino Bill. "That's just Chief Iron Weed. His family has lived on this land for generations, and he's supposed to have magical powers."

"Didn't help keep him out of jail," said the sheriff. "What's he in for?"

"Illegal séance performed by unlicensed practitioner," said Rhino Bill. "Oh, and the mayor was here to see you a while back."

"Doc Holliday? What did he want?"

"Said he wanted to speak to you about leaving Miss Lillie alone or else," said Rhino Bill.

"Or else what?"

"He didn't say."

"I've vowed to shut down his illegal gambling and prostitution enterprises," said Earp, "and I meant it."

"I'd be careful if I was you," said Rhino Bill. "Doc Holliday will carry a grudge to his grave, and he means to have his retribution."

"I'm well aware of his shortcomings," said Earp. "And his strengths. He's very dangerous, and he lacks any compassion for his fellow man."

"Chief?" called Earp. "You OK in there?"

Chief Iron Weed, a member of the Natafus Nation sat on a bunk, looking down at something in his hands. He wore beaten rhino-hide clothing, and his long salt-and-pepper hair was braided into two long plaits that reached his waist.

"OK."

"Listen," Sheriff Earp said, "how about I let you go?"

Looking up, Chief Iron Weed smiled. "I'm surprised to see you here."

"Why is that?"

"The bones," he said, looking back down into his hand.

"What about the bones?"

"The bones tell me your wife is in grave danger, Sheriff. You need to get to her as fast as you can."

"The Brood?" Katie asked. "That's a strange name for children."

"We are Brood," they said with exposed fangs.

"I'm afraid that I think I'd better go," she said, backing away. "I'm not feeling too well tonight. It must have been my fall."

"We are hungry," said the Brood.

"I see," said Katie, reaching behind her for the doorknob. "It's better that I go now. I—"

A small shovel came down squarely on the back of her head, and she fell to the ground but caught herself, her arms extended.

"We need to feed," said the Brood as they circled the fallen Katie.

"No," she begged. "Please…"

One of the smallest, although not the youngest, stepped on her back and pushed her flat to the ground. An older boy reached forward and extinguished the kerosene lamp's flame, allowing darkness to fall over the glass greenhouse as the Brood advanced on their latest prey.

"Stay away from me, you monsters!" Katie screamed.

Pushing them off, she jumped to her feet. Feeling blood oozing from a wound on the back of her head, she opened the door and ran for her life. The Brood gave pursuit. Running on the slippery grass, she fell once before reaching the back door of the mansion. They grabbed at her ankles with their claws and fangs, but she managed to open the door and slam it behind her.

As she ran through the dark kitchen, she hit her leg on a doorframe. Now limping, Katie was almost through the dining room when the Brood burst through the back door and gave chase through the house. They shuffled along quickly, the sound akin to dragging a sack of flour—or dead body—across the floor.

"Stop!" she ordered in the front hallway. "What do you want from me?"

One of the Brood caught up to her and grabbed her by the leg. Katie tried to kick him off, but another boy jumped on her back. Then another grabbed her other leg. She punched the boy and knocked the one on her back into the wall, upon which he fell off. "Hungry!"

Katie reached the front door and seized the knob.

"Feed!"

But the knob would not turn.

The Brood piled on top of her, tearing, clawing, biting, and chewing her body with their bloodsucking kisses until she was no more.

CHAPTER FOUR

Nikki Hale woke up in Katie Earp's bed, screaming.

It was morning.

She got out of bed and realized her nightgown was soaked with sweat. Had she actually witnessed Katie's death, or had it all been just a bad dream? Nikki dressed quickly and went to look for Annie, who'd slept outside on watch. She opened the front door to the daybreak sunshine, and there was Annie Oakley, leaning over a fire and cooking what looked like strips of meat on a grill.

"Smells good," said Nikki. "I'm sorry I slept so long. What time is it?"

She joined Annie by the fire.

"It's still early morning." Annie stood up and offered Nikki some cooked meat. "Did you sleep well?"

"OK," she said, "except for a weird dream I had about Katie Earp that scared the daylights out of me."

"They never found her body," said Annie. "No one—not even the sheriff—is sure she's even dead."

Annie spread out a woven blanket on the ground, its bright native design contrasting sharply with the dull brown dirt. She and Nikki sat down next to the fire. Nikki continued to eat while Annie fed the flames.

"This is good," said Nikki. "What is it?"

"Rhino meat," Annie said. "I think it's the offal."

"Oh, it's pretty good."

Annie giggled innocently.

"What do *you* think?" asked Nikki. "About Katie Earp, I mean."

"I think she's dead," Annie said quickly. "Some say she's living dead, but there ain't no proof of that."

"Living dead?"

"Yeah, declared dead and still alive by feeding on blood."

"You mean like a vampyr?" asked Nikki.

"Vampyr?" asked Annie. "Ain't never heard that before, but Bill did tell me once that those boys were awful peculiar."

"Where I'm from in the future," said Nikki, "a vampyr is a creature that hunts and feeds off warm-blooded mammals—including people—to stay somewhat alive and mobile."

"Mo-bile?"

"Yeah, you know," said Nikki, "able to get around. As a matter of fact, our ancestors were all vampyrs, and they once ruled the earth."

"Really?" asked Annie. "What about if they don't feed?"

"Then they really die, I guess."

"Miss Nikki?" asked Annie. "Are you joshing me?"

"Please, Annie, just Nikki. And no, what I'm telling you is the strange truth."

"Poor Sheriff Earp," said Annie. "He's never gotten over the loss of his dear wife, and to find out she's a...what's it called? Vampyr..."

"Better to stay single," said Nikki. "Fewer feelings to get hurt."

"Not always," said Annie. "Sometimes a loved one can save your life. I know, because it happened to me."

A bolt of lightning shot across the open plains, preceding the ground-rumbling thunder caused by the approaching herds consisting of thousands of wild prairie rhino as they fled several hunters on horseback. The rhino scattered over the fertile plains in all directions as far as the eye could see as the hunters selected the biggest and best specimens to take down and slaughter for meat and hide.

"Don't let those bulls get away!" shouted Rhino Bill Cody, well known for his ability to outmaneuver the escaping herds, pursuing the strongest and most dangerous bull rhinos, knowing the majority of the herd would follow. He spotted a large, one-ton bull on a grassy hill and signaled to the others that he was in pursuit. The rhino, threatened by Cody's approach, charged and managed to wound his horse. Rhino Bill fell off, hit the ground, and rolled to a hard stop against a prairie ant mound. The bull rhino charged, but Rhino Bill managed to roll out of the way. Frustrated, the big bull turned again, stomped its large hooves into the dirt, lowered the sharp horn on its snout, and charged a second time. Unable to move fast enough, Rhino Bill was gored in the leg and dragged over the grassy ground, stuck on the bull's sharp horn, all the way down the sloping terrain.

Bleeding profusely, Rhino Bill tried to break free, but the horn had cut deep, and he wasn't able to dislodge himself from the rhino.

"You OK, Bill?" yelled one of the other hunters on horseback.

"Do I look OK?" asked Rhino Bill. "Stop the rhino!"

The mounted hunter caught up, maneuvering his horse close behind the bull rhino and pulling out his long rifle. Taking aim, he got off two large-shelled shots that blew the back of the rhino's skull off, dropping the great beast to the ground, where it skidded to a stop. Underneath, Rhino Bill lay pinned and barely conscious from the loss of blood. The hunter jumped off his horse while a second hunter rode over to see if he could help.

"Looks bad, Bill," said the hunter. "Not sure what I can do."

"Getting this bloody rhino off me would be a start."

The second hunter dismounted and walked over to the fallen rhino, which was still breathing.

"It's still alive," he shouted.

"Kill it," said Rhino Bill. "Then get a rope around its neck and pull the rhino off me."

"Sure thing, Bill," said one of the hunters closest to the fallen rhino.

He fired a shot from his pistol to end the rhino's life while the other hunter lifted a wound rope off his saddle.

"Bill," he said while tying the rope around the rhino's neck, "it looks like the fall freed your leg from the horn. Hang on, and we'll pull it off you."

"Hurry," said Rhino Bill weakly. "Lost a lot of blood...might pass out."

The hunters worked together to slowly drag the downed rhino off Rhino Bill. He passed out from shock.

"What'll we do now?" asked one of the hunters, bewildered.

The other one looked around the empty prairie.

"We're pretty close to the chief's ancestral home," he said. "Let's take him there."

With that, one of them removed his bandanna and tied it around Rhino Bill's leg to create a tourniquet to stop the bleeding.

"Where did you learn how to do that?" the other asked.

"In the Great War, I was a healer," he said. "I tended the wounded and comforted the dying."

"Where am I?" asked Rhino Bill Cody.

"You're safe," came the faint reply.

He tried to open his eyes, but he was still very weak from his leg wound. All he could see were the blurred outlines of three people sitting around him in a circle.

"I'm here to help you, Bill," said a male voice, "but you need to come with me now."

"Where are we going?" Rhino Bill asked.

"Don't listen to him," a second male voice said. "He's the demon."

"Nonsense," the first male voice said defensively. "I am your salvation!"

"No, leave me be," Rhino Bill tried to say. "I don't want to go with the demon."

"I won't leave without you," the demon said.

"He's lying to you," came the small voice of a female. "That's what demons do."

"Who's there?" Rhino Bill asked.

"My name is Annie Oakley."

"She's taken care of you for three weeks," said the second voice. "I am Chief Iron Weed, and you are in my home."

The ancestral home was actually a large camp located near a wide but shallow river at the base of a mountain. It had been set up there mainly for protection and accessibility. The chief had the largest lodge by far, and there were several smaller lodges for his family and his entourage. A cooker, a toilet, livestock pens, and a ghost lodge lined the river that led to Iron Weed's home.

"Enough of the introductions," snapped the demon. "His sight has returned and this rhino hunter is coming with me."

"You have no power over my dominion," said Chief Iron Weed. "Leave here, demon, before I call down the animal spirits to eat you."

"You don't frighten me, witch," said the scaly, green-gray demon with a wink of his blood-red eye. "This man will join his father in my torment."

"Father?" Rhino Bill asked. "Where is he?"

"Sitting right next to me," said the demon. "Say something to your dying son."

"Boy," said the older man, "are you going to come with us or lie there all day like a little girl?"

"All you ever did was criticize me," said Rhino Bill. "I've been a good son."

"It's not real," said Annie. "It's an illusion conjured up by the demon."

"Clever girl," snarled the demon. "After I'm done dealing with him, I'll cook you on the spit and eat your brains first."

"You'll do no such thing," Chief Iron Weed said. "It's time for you to disappear."

He emptied his bag of small animal bones on Rhino Bill's chest. Waving his hands over the bones, he made strange animal sounds until the bones began to smolder, emitting thick gray smoke into the air.

"Take my hand," Rhino Bill said to Annie.

The bones burst into flames.

Rhino Bill tried to move and shake them off, but he could not.

"What are you doing?" the demon screamed. "The flames—they're burning me!"

Chief Iron Weed waved his hand over the flames, and they turned from a red-yellow hue to a light blue.

"These magical blue flames will cleanse you of the demon's evil spirit inside you and drive it away. Demon, be gone!"

As the flames on Rhino Bill's chest dissipated, so did the demon until he was no more.

"What about his wound?" Annie asked.

"He is healing very rapidly," said Chief Iron Weed. "His heart is strong."

"How bad is it?" asked Rhino Bill.

"Show him," said Chief Iron Weed.

Annie rolled back the bandages from around Rhino Bill's leg and showed him a long, jagged vertical wound, now stitched together with some type of organic matter that looked like tree vine.

"The bull's horn cut deep," said Chief Iron Weed, "and in places it cut into the bone. I'm afraid the damage is so severe your days of hunting wild rhinos are over. You can wrap his leg now, Annie."

"Thank you for being honest with me, Chief," said Rhino Bill. "I have a lot to think about."

"You should be up and walking fine in about six weeks. In the meantime, Annie is an excellent caregiver and companion. She'll get you well."

Annie picked up a new bandage and rolled it tightly around his leg.

"There is something else I'd like to talk to you about," said Chief Iron Weed. "Something I sense inside you. You have the gift. Have you ever witnessed anything unusual?"

"You mean dead people?"

"Yes."

"When I was a kid," Rhino Bill said, "I saw my grandparents, dead more than ten years, standing in a field and motioning for me to come join them. That week I almost drowned in a flash flood."

"And now?" the chief asked him.

"Now I only see what's real and leave the world of the dead to the experts like you."

"Pity," said Chief Iron Weed. "But now I must go and tend to some other tribal business."

He left, leaving Rhino Bill alone with Annie.

"How old are you, anyway?" he asked.

"Eleven," Annie said. "But I'm very mature for my age."

"Come on, Annie," Nikki said. "Admit it—you saved Bill's life, so when did he save yours?"

"That came later," she said, "after we left Chief Iron Weed and started hunting ghosts."

"I hope you're not offended by my asking this," said Nikki, "but you were eleven years old when you met Bill, right?"

"Around there," said Annie. "I ain't really sure of my exact age."

Nikki helped put out the fire, and they packed up and moved back inside the house.

"I mean, I was pretty wild at an early age," said Nikki, "and I now think that was way too young."

"I'm not sure what you mean," Annie said. "You talk real fast."

"Uh...Bill's much older than you, Annie," said Nikki. "You're young and have so many years ahead of you to really figure out what you want."

"I already figured it out, Nikki," Annie said. "That's why I married Bill."

"You're married?"

"Yep," Annie said. "Got hitched when I turned fifteen."

Back inside the sheriff's house, Nikki began to feel unsettled about her situation.

"It's time to get going," said Annie. "The sheriff said to bring you into town by noon, after you were rested and fed."

"Like his horse," said Nikki, smirking. "Modern women don't take orders like that."

"You're funny," said Annie, who carried her rifle everywhere she went. "The sheriff doesn't think you're a horse. As a matter of fact, I think he's sweet on you."

"I guess I have a lot to learn," said Nikki. "Things happen much slower in this era, and the times are much more violent. Emotions are so raw and public. Where I come from—"

"Well, we'd better not keep the sheriff waiting," said Annie. "He's not the patient type."

Nikki stepped out into the sunlight, shut the door behind her, stopped abruptly, and turned to Annie.

"So, Annie...tell me," Nikki said. "What is the legal age under current law for getting married in this quadrant?"

"Twelve."

CHAPTER FIVE

"I don't know about you, Annie," said Nikki Hale, "but I find the sheriff's house so depressing! No wonder he's so sad and lonely."

"I think that's why you're here," said Annie Oakley. "To cheer him up."

"Well, keep that to yourself, Annie," said Nikki. "I'm just trying to find a way back to my own time."

Nikki, driving a one-horse carriage borrowed from Earp's stable, followed Annie on horseback into Ghost Town. They turned down Main Street and stopped in front of the town's jail. The women secured their horses and headed inside.

Its walls were painted jailhouse gray, and its spartan furniture included a desk and chair in the office, two bunks in two cells in the back, and a stove to fix coffee and grub.

Nikki sat down in the sheriff's chair by the desk. Annie stood behind her.

"How long have you lived in Ghost Town, Annie?" asked Nikki.

"Ever since Bill and me came here to fight ghosts."

"Everyone seems to have a ghost story," Nikki said. "I've had bad dreams, but really, I don't think—"

"Ghost Town is haunted, Nikki," said Annie. "It's a feeling of being watched everywhere you go."

"Yeah, I do feel that," said Nikki, "but I'm not sure it's about ghosts."

"Truth be told," said Anne, "I didn't really want to come here. I'd heard stories about Ghost Town from hunters who passed through the chief's camp. After the cave-in disaster, the stories turned from gold to ghosts, and it really shook up lots of people—including me."

"Do you remember the gold bust, Annie?"

"No," she said. "But the chief told me about it when I was a child."

"Tell me," said Nikki. "What was it like?"

"He said it was bittersweet."

The gold rush started with an indigenous boy, and it ended seven years later with an explosion at a major gold mine that buried alive all thirty-five miners at work that day.

Before gold was discovered in the mountains, the indigenous population had lived on the land for generations. They had aided the first settlers who arrived in the fertile plains between the mountains, sharing food and shelter so that they could survive through the first bitterly cold winter. Without help from the indigenous people, the settlers would have perished. But once they were firmly established, the settlers thrived. They built permanent homes to live in and a general store to serve the area's new population, and farmers raised domesticated rhino and prairie chickens for sale and slaughter. As it prospered, the new settlement of Hope, as it was then called, was loosely governed by a group of its elders, who one day decided to throw a big party to celebrate their good fortune. No expense was spared, even the indigenous people contributed, and the festivities took place in the settlement's largest building: the grain hall built to hold feed and livestock. All the new settlement folk, dressed in their prairie finest, drank a peyote extract concoction and mingled with the native born to celebrate their prosperity. Gunshots were fired. Fire dancing, rhino calf roping and riding, and a Miss Hope beauty contest were among the events planned. After a few speeches of self-congratulation by the elders, a young indigenous boy, perhaps no more than ten years old, walked forward to the long table where the elders were seated. Startled at first by the boy's aggressive move toward them, the elders soon turned their attention to what he pulled out of his pocket.

"What have you there, boy?" asked one of the slightly intoxicated elders. "What are you carrying?"

"A gift for the new town of Hope," said the young boy. "From my people."

"Well," said another of the elders, "don't just stand there all day. Show us!"

"I bring you a shiny rock from the mountain," said the indigenous boy and held out his hand.

The elders looked confused.

"Is that gold?" asked a short, stout elder.

"Gold!" shouted another elder.

"Gold!" the elders all muttered, realizing its value.

"I want a closer look," one of the elders said, getting up and walking over toward the boy. He took the shiny stone from the boy's hand and rolled it around in his own.

"And you found this on the mountain?" he asked as he examined the stone. "Was it just lying on the ground?"

"I found it in a cave," said the boy. "I have more."

"More?" a senior elder asked, grinning with glee.

Everyone in the room grew silent.

The indigenous boy dug into his other pocket and pulled out a second large, shiny stone. A few more of the elders rose and quickly made their way to the boy, vying to be the first to reach for the gold.

"You mentioned a cave?" asked the elder, plucking the largest stone. "Where is it?"

"At the bottom of the big mountain, under a hanging cliff," the boy said.

"Yes," said another elder, "but where *exactly?*"

"These shiny stones are a gift from my people," the boy said. "The rest belongs to us, and its location is our secret."

"We have no use for secrets here," muttered the short, stout elder, who had remained seated. "Not at all."

"Oh, no," chorused the other elders.

"Come now, boy," another elder said, impatiently. "Tell us where the gold can be found."

"What is this gold, as you call it?" asked the boy.

"Those shiny rocks you brought us," said the elder. "This is gold, and it has a very high monetary value."

"Monetary?" asked the indigenous boy. He turned and looked at his people, who stood near the back of the room. One of them motioned for him to come, but he was stopped from leaving by an elder who grabbed him. Other indigenous men moved forward and shielded the boy, guiding him safely out of the hall.

"We must stop them," said an elder. "And take the gold...it's wasted on them."

After that day, relations between the indigenous people and the new settlers grew tense, and the gift of gold turned into a curse. They ignored each other at first, but then the gold fever became too much for the elders, and they declared war and marched on the indigenous people's camp by the river. The battle was bloody, and many of the indigenous people died. The ones who survived were marched back to town for punishment.

One of those captured was their leader, Chief Iron Weed, who begged the elders to not hurt any more of his people. But his pleas fell on deaf ears—the new settlers wanted the gold, and all they thought about was getting more. When they arrived back at the settlement, the prisoners were tied to tall cut-pine posts that had been placed in the ground earlier in the day. Surrounding them were bundles of twigs and dried grasses placed at their feet by the settler children, who giggled as they watched one of the elders hold a lit torch to the bundles one by one, until all were burned alive.

Only Chief Iron Weed was spared to witness their cruelty, forced to watch as his own family was destroyed. Broken, he told them where the gold could be found, and fever turned to madness for the people of Hope. Men, women, and children abandoned their livestock and crops in order to prospect full time. Entire families searched the mountains from dawn until dusk, looking for caves that might hold golden nuggets the size of a clenched fist. Before long, without proper attention, their crops failed, and the livestock wandered off to join the wild herds that lived beyond the valley. The settlers soon grew hungry and desperate.

Forced to watch his people killed and abused, Chief Iron Weed vowed revenge. "I curse you all with horrific deaths at the hands of our ancestor spirits."

The elders, ignoring their own people's cries for food, did manage to find gold using prisoners and criminals they hired and even set up a mining operation, and the profits soon poured in, though it was not shared equally among the townsfolk who'd driven off the indigenous people. The profits were sent to bankers back east, where they were held in the elders' names and pocketbooks. It was the elders who decided to rebuild the settlement of Hope into a real town that was better suited to the needs of the newly wealthy.

In place of the grain hall, a woman named Lillie Langtrees opened a fancy saloon featuring dancing girls and a brothel upstairs and out back.

Miss Lillie's saloon and brothel became the most visited places in the new town, which doubled in size within two years—and so did its crime rate, thanks to the criminals the elders had brought in to mine. The arrival of more and more young, hard-drinking men led to fights over claims, women, and ego that would sometimes end in death. Killings, robberies, gunfights, public lewdness, and claim jumping all became common practice when more of the criminal element moved into town, lured by the new wealth, lax leadership, and busy prostitutes flush with gold. The town's death rate also rose, and the ordinary citizens began to despair. When the elders realized that crime was out of control, they sent out an urgent message back east to hire a lawman.

The first one who showed up was Sheriff Wyatt Earp, a military veteran of the Great War and the associate sheriff from Tombstone who'd cleaned up several towns with his fast gun and persuasive personality. Upon finding the advertisement, he applied for the sheriff's job using the telewire, the latest discovery from the secretive inventor Alex G. Bell. The telewire was a new mode of communication that involved a series of electrical impulses that Bell turned into readable code that traveled along miles of wires strung between cities on the east coast and the west.

Earp had been hired on the spot, and his responsibilities included guarding the jail, patrolling the town perimeter, and officiating at weddings. After about a year on the job, he was able to push out the most brutal criminal elements, sparking a serious drop in crime that made most of the townsfolk happy.

But not everyone celebrated.

Some of the town's citizens had prospered from the crime surrounding the gold trade and were not happy with the new sheriff, who'd put a dent in their profits.

One individual who kept his distance was the town's mortician, who went by the name of Doc Holliday. Doc's family had been part of the original settler group in the valley, and he'd inherited his father's wealth and control over the town's transportation routes. Nothing entered or left the town without Doc's family getting a cut. He'd been a spoiled boy who treated the servants like slaves and tortured his pets. Later, he received degrees in chemistry and alchemy from a major university back east, but he eventually found an interest in taxidermy and then went into the mortician trade back home. He even got himself elected mayor, a position that functioned as a front for his more nefarious activities. Through a series of questionable transactions, he ended up owning the largest-producing gold mine outside town and, like the elders before him, used indebted miners and criminal labor to dig for gold.

His partner in crime was the diminutive saloonkeeper Lillie Langtrees. She ran the financial side of the business and laundered Doc Holliday's profits by buying up the town's real estate.

Earp was a threat to their plans, because he was not susceptible to their threats and could not be bought—not even with gold.

Gold became the currency of the day. It was all anyone would talk about—finding it, mining it, and spending the wealth on themselves and their families. Farming and herding gave way to mining and banking. Women's button-up shoes sold out at Miss Windi's clothing emporium. Babies began to appear with their parents on the streets after years of infertility. Outsiders moved in, building extravagant homes and stables. There was even talk coming from the capital, Washington, DC, that the railroad was extending west through the center of Hope on its way to the coast. A railroad station with indoor plumbing and solar fans was quickly built, funded by donations from the wealthy gold-mining families in town who pulled all the strings. Prosperity was at hand—yet a dark cloud hung over the western mountains, where the surviving indigenous people had been forced to hide. There, in caves, they danced around fires, calling up ancient demons to bring down their wrath against the usurpers of their lands. Magic became their currency, and, led by Chief Iron Weed, who called in faraway family to replenish his tribe, they cast multiple spells in the old language of the Ancients to destroy the new settlers and put an end to their golden age.

Then the unthinkable happened. A never-explained explosion occurred in the mountains near one of the richest gold mines, one that produced several ounces of gold each day, shaking its foundation and causing the framework to buckle and collapse. Thirty-five miners were trapped miles underneath the ground, their air supply cut off.

The elders seemed confused and were unable to provide any

coherent direction or a rescue plan. Two of them committed suicide, by hanging themselves from a tree limb.

Frustrated, Earp deputized a few of the townsfolk, and they went into the mountains to rescue the gold miners, but they soon realized it was hopeless—there was no physical way for them to move giant rocks and tons of dirt alone. Explosives were tried, but this only made matters worse. After a few days without success, the gold mine became a mass grave.

"They say this place is cursed," said an elder who eventually showed up at the miners' grave, "because we took the gold from their people."

"Superstition," said Earp. "The miners could still be alive. We at least have to try."

"I believe they are dead already, sheriff," said the elder. "There is nothing you can do."

He walked away down the hill.

The cave-in soured the frightened populace on gold mining. The price of gold dropped almost immediately, and young prospectors, until then the town's lifeblood, stopped coming. The downtrend in price bankrupted the rest of the miners and affected every business and the many individuals up and down the food chain who catered to their needs. The gold boom turned into a bust, and the town of Hope did not survive.

"Yes," said Nikki, "that's quite a story, but that still doesn't explain how Rhino Bill saved your life."

"One day," Annie said, "just after sunset when you could still see clearly, I was wandering around the old train station looking for ghosts, and there, about ten feet in front of me, appeared five long-dead miners wearing their dirty work overalls and holding unlit cave lanterns in their hands. Their faces were torn and gray-colored, and they had no eyes, just empty sockets. I was shocked—not because I'd never seen a ghost before, but just that they'd caught me off guard."

"Stay calm," said Rhino Bill, who appeared as if by magic behind Annie. "Do not make any sudden moves."

Screech!

A large, black-feathered raven called from a tall pine tree high above their heads and flapped its wings.

"Yes, I hear you, Cousin," said Rhino Bill as he looked up. "Tell me, what's happening here?"

The large black bird flapped its wings in sequential motions for a few moments and then screeched again loudly.

"Thank you, Cousin," Rhino Bill said. "Now I know the way."

The sky grew dark as the last vestiges of daylight left the prairie.

Rhino Bill stepped in front of Annie and pulled a small silver flask from his vest pocket. The miners seemed to come alive at the sight of the flask and moved slowly toward Rhino Bill and Annie. Rhino Bill opened the cap and held it in his hand.

"It's time for you to leave this place," he commanded as blue smoke rose from the flask and seemed to hover in the air. The miners started shaking but continued to stagger forward. "You will follow the sound of my voice and enter the everlasting void."

"We not obey," the five miners said in unison, even the one missing a lower jaw. "Want revenge for death."

"The town was not responsible," said Annie. "The cave-in was an accident."

"An accident…paid with our lives."

"You have no place here," said Rhino Bill, shaking liquid from the flask onto the approaching miners. "If you follow me, you'll find peace."

Skeletal or not, they were approaching quite fast. But Rhino Bill's action had little effect. One of the skeletons ignited its lantern and broke off from the others. It passed Rhino Bill and grabbed Annie, who had no opportunity to get off a shot.

"No peace!" it said. "This place—this ghost town—will forever be haunted."

Annie tried to break free as the miner raised the lantern to its face and revealed the twisting earthworms that slithered out of its eye, ear, and nose sockets.

"Stay calm," said Rhino Bill. "The bird told me the worst is yet to come."

"Calm?" replied Annie, who swiftly broke free with a kick to the skull and used the butt of her gun to smash in the miner's face. Rhino Bill fought off three miners that had surrounded him, using a long knife and his rifle butt, breaking them into body parts that littered the ground. Annie shot the fifth miner through its neck, shattering the spine and allowing the head to separate and fall.

"Nice!" said Rhino Bill as he splashed the liquid over the body parts. They promptly disintegrated into the ground.

"What is that stuff, anyway?" asked Annie.

"Just aftershave," said Rhino Bill. "But it usually gets the job done."

They'd started to walk away from the railroad station and up Main Street when out from behind several buildings came more dead miners, fifteen in all—different shapes, sizes, and colors, some missing body parts, some with deep facial wounds, and some with bones protruding from their bodies, teeth marks showing they'd been chewed on.

"The bird didn't say anything about this," said Rhino Bill.

"It said the worst was yet to come," said Annie. "Well, I guess that's what it meant."

The miners moved forward toward Main Street with clumsy, doll-like motions, their arms outstretched, putting one leg in front of the other and their mouths snapping like turtles.

"They're heading for the center of town," said Annie. She fired her rifle multiple times, but the bullets just passed through the spectral miners' bodies and hit the trees behind them.

"Hey!" she said. "How come the other ones weren't like this?"

The miners' ghosts kept moving toward them.

"These are real ghosts," said Rhino Bill. "Them others were walking corpses."

The slow-moving ghosts split into groups as they approached, one half reaching for Annie and the other half heading for Rhino Bill.

"If you're going to do anything, Bill," said Annie, "you'd better do it now."

"I've run out of aftershave," Rhino Bill said. "But I do have another trick up my sleeve. Birds."

"Birds?"

"Ghosts are afraid of birds," he said. "Especially black birds."

The dead miners reached Annie, and, able to touch but not be touched, they ripped Annie's shirt and tugged at her boots. They lifted her up over their heads and carried her forward as she screamed for help.

"Cousin, I need your help!" called Rhino Bill between bouts of swinging his fists through the miners' ghosts.

The large, dark raven swooped down from its perch, leading a flock of about fifty blackbirds that descended from the surrounding trees and swarmed the ghosts, freeing Annie and Rhino Bill. The birds flashed and fluttered so quickly around the spectral bodies that a vortex was created that literally tore the ghosts to shreds, leaving nothing but dust behind.

"And that's how Rhino Bill saved my life."

CHAPTER SIX

Mayor and mortician Doc Holliday—a short, balding man who had long sideburns that formed a beard, wore ill-fitting, worn-out suits, and had large appetites both for food and women—looked out the window from his run-down office above the dilapidated general store on Main Street and pondered his good fortune. Soon he would have his revenge on the one man responsible, he believed, for his miserable life in Ghost Town. He'd been elected mayor because his family, along with other early settlers' families, owned most of the land that had been taken from the indigenous peoples when they arrived. His father had also been mayor and had made his fortune in the land speculation business that had uprooted entire nations from their ancestral lands.

As a child, Holliday had been taught to trust no one and always make the choice that returned the most profit. Today, his focus was on building a bomb—one powerful enough to blow up the whole town if he wanted to.

Holliday liked to play with explosives. He'd started at an early age with matches and had burned down several homes by design. His interest in arson led to a fascination with gunpowder, and by the time he was a teen, he had destroyed many buildings on his father's land, some which may have been occupied by his extended family, in order to test the killing power of his latest bombs. But the thing he couldn't control was the timing of the bombs. What Holliday needed was a way to trigger an explosion from a distance.

He also liked dead things. As a youngster, Holliday would capture small animals for torture. He'd light them on fire or blow them up and then stuff their hides with leaves, dirt, and gunpowder to create otherworldly shaped creatures. He would play with these monstrosities for hours on end—or until the creatures fell apart.

Sent away to boarding school back east, he was a loner who didn't have any friends and never became accustomed to the cooler eastern climate and its more aggressive populace. He kept to himself, living alone in a boarding house off campus and only going out at night to collect dead animals off the road. Taxidermy took up most of his time. He failed almost all his other subjects in school, where he had few interests beyond the study of chemistry. Holliday used his taxidermy skills to get a part time job in the morgue, where he cleaned corpses while working the graveyard shift. Most people would be uneasy around so many dead, but it fascinated Holliday, and he used care with every body he touched. He'd often hold their hands, wondering about their lives prior to their arrival at the morgue. Sometimes when he was working the shift by himself, he'd pull out all the bodies and line them up based on his own idea of a perfect family. He would talk to them as if they were still alive, but they never answered back.

Late one night, a man approached Holliday at the entrance to the morgue and inquired about purchasing the bodies of the recently dead for use in research. The man—a tall, shadowy figure wearing a long, dark-maroon cloak and hood—wanted to remain anonymous but told Holliday he belonged to a secret society known as the Resurrectionists. As a group, they collected fresh, recently deceased bodies and then sold them for profit to hospitals and universities, where they were used for research and education. Holliday was reluctant. His salary from the morgue covered his living expenses, and his family paid for school. He turned the hooded man down.

The next week, everything changed for Holliday. In a letter, his father wrote the following:

Dear Son,

I hope you are well and have finally adjusted to your new life back east. I know it's a tiresome place, but opportunity is much greater there—especially for someone with your limited skills. Things are not good here at home. Your mother continues to spend money I don't have, buying things she does not need—clothes, furnishings, art. Truth be told, I myself have lost a lot of money playing cards, placing bets on the ponies, and fixing local boxing matches. My good fortune has turned, son, and I've had to borrow from friends and relatives. I even took out a loan from a big bank back east.

That is the reason for this letter—to inform you that the bank has called in my loan early, and since I have no money, I am also unable to continue to pay your school tuition. I'm sorry to have to write this letter, but the family is in a shambles, and both your mother and I spend most of our time with drink. My disposition has soured, and I hold one man responsible for our family's tragic fate. His name is James A. Garfield, and he is a young banker who talked me into the loan that I now cannot repay. Don't be fooled—this scoundrel is a dangerous man, but he's a man nonetheless, and he can be stopped. You, my faithful son, must avenge our family's name and destroy this evil, greedy man who destroyed us.

With much love,
Your father, Joshua

With no savings of his own, Holliday had no choice but to accept the Resurrectionist's offer, and he began to exchange bodies from the morgue for food on the table.

The maroon-cloaked and hooded men who appeared to pick up the packages wrapped in brown paper were still a mystery to Holliday, and he liked it that way.

"We want you to attend one of our meetings," said the robed Resurrectionist, who appeared one evening and spoke to him, which was a rarity. "We'd like you to get to know us better."

"I don't want to know you better," said Holliday, "or what happens to the bodies I give you. This is strictly a financial arrangement. Understood?"

"Yes," the Resurrectionist said. "We will agree to your wishes."

"I'll bet you have little choice," said Holliday. "Unless you harvest your own bodies."

"We're merchants," the Resurrectionist said. "We leave the dirty work up to others, like you."

Holliday started out slowly but soon found there was a huge demand for cadavers. So he located an unlimited supply in the poorer districts of the city, where the early-childhood and senior-related deaths provided ample inventory for his customers. At night, he spent hours dismembering the lost and less fortunate, packaging them into neatly wrapped rectangles about a foot in length and tied with natural cord, ready for travel to their destination by wagon.

The increased demand also enabled him to continue his academic studies in both chemistry and taxidermy. Within two years, he'd earned enough to fully own the morgue and expand, building a strong business based on selling the dead. For the first time in his life, Holliday was an independent man in his twenties and able to live comfortably in an east coast environment he despised. Having no interpersonal skills, he remained alone and frequently visited prostitutes for pleasure, preferring to spend the majority of his time expanding the body business by acquiring neighboring morgues.

Even success could not sway Holliday from his goal, the one his father had requested in his letter, and he spent a small fortune getting closer to the target—the young banker James A. Garfield, who held the blame for the Holliday family's misfortune.

CHAPTER SEVEN

James A. Garfield, Leader of Nena Continent, was a fair and honest yet very ambitious young man. Dirt poor by birth, he joined the continent's army as a teen and rose up the ranks to general. Afterward, he attended college on scholarship, earning degrees in warfare and social service, and then spent years as a banking and finance professional, building his profile in the capital of Nena, Washington, DC. Thereafter, Garfield burst onto the political scene like a rocket with the backing of the eastern bloc and was elected legislator of his district, which included the whole eastern seaboard. Not long after that, he became Vice Leader as a reward for streamlining the continental banking system. Finally, he was elected Leader after a group known as the Anarchists assassinated his predecessor.

Garfield resided on a tree-lined street in DC, where one or two large houses took up most of the neighborhood lots. His family consisted of his lovely wife, Lucretia, and their twin baby boys, Harry Augustus and James Jr. They lived in the old part of town in a big redbrick house with a white porch fronted by three giant oak trees and numerous bodyguards stationed around the block. The household also included three servants: Joanna, the house-keeper; Dalia, the cook; and Roger, the butler, and head of staff.

Juanita Redmond, Lucretia's mother and Garfield's mother-in-law, who lived with the family and looked after the babies while Lucretia rested, wore her hair up in a bun, was tube slim, and was very superstitious. Living through the Great War, she was an anxious woman who trusted no one, not even her daughter, Lucretia. Always fearing the worst, she was overly protective of her grandchildren and would take them out only under her own supervision.

Daily walks became a routine. Juanita left the house every day at ten in the morning to take the twins in their double pram to the park down the block for what she said was the freshest of air.

Someone noticed the pattern.

Doc Holliday had taken lodgings at a hotel around the corner from Garfield's residence. His campaign of fear and intimidation began with the mother-in-law. Each morning, he left his hotel room and walked toward Garfield's house, sometimes stopping to speak with the neighbors, who gladly told him everything he wanted to know about the family living in the redbrick house, including the number of bodyguards they employed. He found out, for instance, that Roger, the fastidious butler, had been given a military discharge during the Great War for unnatural behavior.

Holliday would eventually reach the park, where he would follow Juanita and the twins around for weeks, noting their usual route, the time they spent, and the fact that she bought the same ice-cream flavor every day: strawberry. After she'd return home with the babies in the double pram, Holliday would continue to walk back to his hotel, where he would write threatening letters to Leader Garfield about the kidnapping and murder of his wife and twin sons.

On the street one day, Holliday approached Juanita on her daily stroll with the twins, asked her for directions, and then made small talk about the weather, her clothing, and the riffraff playing in the park that day—all the while keeping his eye on the babies in the double pram. Suspicious at first, Juanita became charmed by his attention and soon dropped her guard altogether.

What a pleasant man, Juanita thought. He's so well mannered.

They walked on together, and Holliday offered to push the pram. She obliged and took his arm to steady herself as they walked, looking into his eyes coquettishly and smiling. It had been a while since Juanita had shared the company of a young man, and this one was so polite. They rounded a cobblestone path hidden behind some giant willow trees near the lake where most people did not venture and stopped. Holliday looked around and then took a deep breath.

"Why have we stopped?" Juanita asked, nervously.

He did not answer. Suddenly he reached out and grabbed her by the throat with both hands, squeezing as hard as he could. She tried to struggle, but it didn't last long. Her face turned blue and then white as the life drained out of her. She fell to the ground, dead.

Holliday dragged Juanita's body behind one of the willow trees almost to the edge of the lake. There, he took off his shoes and socks, rolled up his pant legs, and waded into the water, dragging Juanita's body into the lake at least ten feet offshore. He briefly left the body to go back to shore for some large rocks to weigh her down. When he was done, her body successfully submerged, he walked back to shore, put on his shoes and socks, and walked back to the cobblestone path. The twins in the double pram began to cry, one inciting the other.

"Shush, little babies," he said, standing in front of them. "You won't miss her a bit."

Holliday pushed the double pram forward down the path, and the rocking motion put the babies back to sleep.

Roger, the Garfields' butler, was a more personal target of Holliday's plan. Detectives he hired discovered that Roger had been undesirably discharged from the armed forces due to the practice of deviant behavior. Holliday planned to use the information to blackmail Roger into becoming his eyes and ears inside the Garfield home.

"Excuse me," Holliday said to Roger one day on the street outside their residence. "I'm covering the disappearance of the woman in the park for the press. Tell me, sir, do you think the woman is still alive?"

"We're not allowed to speak to the press," said Roger. "Sir's orders."

"I'm not really with the press." Holliday smiled. "You're just so good-looking that I wanted a way to meet you."

"You think I'm attractive?" asked Roger.

"Yes. Very."

"Well, it may have been true once," Roger said with a sigh, "but now I'm older. I must work for a living."

"You are still a very handsome man," said Holliday. "So, tell me, where do you think the mother-in-law ended up?"

Roger looked squarely into Holliday's eyes.

"No one knows," Roger quietly replied. "The old bag was a pain, anyway, so I'm not surprised someone would murder her."

"Murder?" said Holliday. "I thought the papers said she was just missing."

"The authorities think she's been murdered," said Roger. "They found the double pram near the entrance to the park, and the twins unharmed. She never would have left it there if she were still alive."

"Have they found the body yet?" asked Holliday, nonchalantly.

"Roger," he said. "My name is Roger."

"And mine is Smith," Holliday said with a smile, extending his hand to shake. "Andrew Smith, but everybody calls me Andy."

"No, they haven't found her body," said Roger, "but it's just a matter of time."

Juanita Redmond was already long gone. Her body had been

fished from the lake later the night of her murder by members of the Resurrectionists, dried off, carved up, and shipped to various medical research facilities, where they were working on cures for Ebola, polio, and the common cold.

Roger was smitten with Holliday and visited him frequently during the week at his hotel, where, after a lot of heavy drink, they'd have intimate conversations about the Garfield household, including his neurotic wife Lucretia, who couldn't, or wouldn't take care of her two babies, possible financial trouble, and a missing, assumed-dead mother-in-law whom no one wanted back.

Unbeknownst to Holliday, *his* presence had not gone unnoticed. He was seen around the Garfield home once too often by the local authorities and soon became a suspect in the missing-person case of Garfield's mother-in-law, Juanita. Witnesses came forward stating they'd seen a short man walking with a woman dressed in gray pushing a baby's double pram. Holliday was taken down to the police station for questioning, but without a body and no evidence other than hearsay, they had to let him go.

Unshaken, he continued executing his plan to destroy Garfield and his family that had started with the strangulation of Juanita and would eventually end in the deaths of them all, but he needed Roger's help to betray his employer and set the trap.

Roger refused to get involved until Holliday threatened to go public with evidence of his sexual orientation and other proclivities that had gotten him thrown out of the military. Unless he agreed to plant a bomb Holliday crudely built—filled with sharp nails, crushed glass, jagged pieces of metal, and small stones—Roger's reputation would be ruined. That meant he would lose his job, his security, and his remaining self-respect. Roger felt he had no choice, but he told Holliday that he couldn't guarantee his silence if he were caught with the device—not without being given compensation. Holliday decided to kill Roger after his usefulness ended.

A few days later, Holliday gave the bomb—placed in a straw suitcase, fashionable at the time—to Roger, who took it out of the hotel and unsteadily walked it down the street to the Garfield home. The suitcase weighed around fifteen pounds, and about halfway to his destination, Roger had to place it down for a few moments before resuming his walk.

What Holliday had failed to tell Roger was that the bomb he carried was on a timer and set to go off in ten minutes—enough time for him to reach the house and lay the suitcase in the dining room where Garfield ate lunch with his family every day at noon. In his hotel room, Holliday waited for the sound of the explosion, eagerly anticipating his revenge against Garfield for destroying his family. His father had committed suicide, and his mother had drunk herself to death.

Killing this man, he thought, will make me feel whole.

He waited.

And he waited.

No explosion.

He glanced at the clock. It was past ten minutes. Something must have gone wrong.

It had. At the last minute, Roger had gotten cold feet. He'd left the suitcase on the ground and ran off, never to be heard from again. The suitcase had fallen over from its own weight and broken open, exposing the guts of the bomb. The fall must have dislodged some of Holliday's handiwork, as the broken-in-two bomb did not explode. The neighbors were horrified and demanded an investigation into how an undetonated bomb had been found in their posh neighborhood. After the discovery of the bomb right outside his own house, Garfield hired more bodyguards and now commanded a small army. Already a suspect in the disappearance of Juanita, Holliday was picked up and taken to police headquarters in downtown Washington, DC, where he was thrown in with other suspects, cross-examined by hard-core cops, and held overnight, whereupon he was uncuffed, driven to the train station without being given time to gather up his belongings, and thrown onto a train heading west—back where he'd come from, disgraced and nearly broke.

Years later, Doc Holliday sat in his office above the general store and stared out the window to the prairie. There was a knock on the door.

"Yes?" he asked. "Who is it?"

"It's me—Lillie."

Saloon keeper, entertainer, and brothel madam, Lillie Langtrees had what was known as marriage of convenience with the mayor and mortician, Doc Holliday. He funded her operations, got a cut of the saloon and brothel businesses, and kept the law off her back. He was also infatuated with her, and, knowing this, she used it to get her way with him.

"I'm so glad you're here," said Holliday. "You don't come around much anymore. I'm hurt."

Lillie walked into the near-empty office and looked around for a place to sit.

"When are you going to furnish this place?" she asked. "There's not even a clean chair here for a lady to sit down in."

"Please take my seat, Lillie," he said. "I prefer to stand."

She sat down and crossed her hands on her lap.

"Now, what can I do for you?" he asked.

"I'm here because I found out you're cheating me," Lillie said.

"Don't be coy," Holliday said. "Tell me how you really feel."

"Must we play this silly game every time we talk business?" she asked.

"Must we always talk about business?" he said, reproachfully. "I was hoping you'd come here for more personal reasons."

Lillie rolled her eyes. "Back to the cheating," she said. "I've been supplying the girls you asked for, and you still haven't paid me for the last six months' supply. I know you're not broke, and I know about your little side business with the Resurrectionists. I just want what's mine."

"I've had a few financial setbacks lately."

"That's not my concern," she said. "I have to pay my own bills. Either pay up or no more free rides."

"I don't like it when you play the harsh little businesswoman," he said. "I prefer your feminine charms—a whiff of your latest perfume, a speck of face powder, and those lovely ruby-red lips."

"We also need to talk about the sheriff," she said. "You're supposed to be protecting me from him, but it's not working."

"He shouldn't worry you," said Holliday. "He's a peasant, and you... you, my dear, are a queen!"

"The sheriff has been hanging around the saloon with his deputy almost every night, asking the girls questions. I've seen him talking to the bartenders and even the kitchen help. What if he finds out what we're up to? I want it to stop."

"Anything you ask, my darling," he said. "As mayor of Ghost Town, I am Earp's boss, and if I say not to bother you, he won't bother you."

"How can you be so sure?"

"Because Earp is ex-military. He follows orders. Now, let's stop all this complicated business talk. Give me a kiss."

"I'd rather kiss a cactus," she said as she got up from her seat. "How are you going to stop him?"

"Don't you worry your pretty little head about that, Lillie. I've got a plan to rid us of both Earp and Leader Garfield at the same time."

"Garfield?" she asked, surprised.

"It's a long story," he said. "He and I go way back, before he was the Leader of Nena Continent."

"And what makes you think it will be so easy to take out the Leader?" she asked. "He's protected by twenty-four-hour guards."

"I have a secret weapon," he said. "An inventor named Alex G. Bell has discovered a way to detonate bombs from long distances using the earth's magnetic waves."

"I don't have your education," said Lillie.

"Basically, I could detonate a bomb placed near Garfield from miles away," he said. "Get it? His guards won't be able to stop it, and they'll be killed themselves."

"This Bell," said Lillie. "Can he be trusted?"

"He owes me a lot of money," said Holliday. "He foolishly borrowed to finance another of his crackpot inventions. He'll do whatever I tell him."

"In the meantime," she said, "Earp is still nosing around my saloon."

"Be patient, my lovely Lillie," Holliday said. "That do-gooder Earp and the Leader of this nation, Garfield, will soon no longer be a threat to either one of us."

Holliday moved toward Lillie.

"Now, how about that kiss?"

CHAPTER EIGHT

Meanwhile, back east in Washington, DC, the Leader's wife, Lucretia, had put the Garfield twins to bed herself and then fallen asleep in the library, reading in a comfy chair. The clock on the mantel chimed at midnight, and all was quiet in the house. Not a creature was stirring, not even…

"Right this way, sir," said Watson, the new butler.

Quietly, Leader Garfield walked from a room upstairs to the newly installed lift that was powered by electric current. Watson followed, shutting the metal cage door behind them, and then the lift began to descend to the basement, where a nightclub cabaret had been built to the Leader's specifications. The nightclub was at least three thousand square feet and had a stage with a long red velvet curtain with gold braid tassels hanging on each end. The stage was fronted by café tables and single chairs placed throughout the space. Gaslights glowed above a long mahogany bar that went from one end of the room to the other, and the new electric-current lights in chandeliers dropped from the tin ceiling, giving the room a warm glow.

The doors to the lift opened, and the Leader emerged, stopped for a second, and looked around the room.

"No need to worry, sir," said Watson. "The crowd has yet to gather."

Watson was a tall, stout man who wore a colorful pinstriped vest over a white shirt, gray slacks, and shiny black dress shoes. His face was familiar, with its twisted handlebar mustache and long gray-white beard capped by his balding head.

"Very good, Watson," the Leader Garfield said. "You know what they say—the show must go on."

"Indeed, sir," Watson said. "I would agree."

Garfield, followed by Watson, made his way backstage to a small dressing room that contained a padded chair, a small table holding a pearl-colored case, and a large framed mirror leaning against the wall.

The Leader took off his suit jacket and handed it to Watson, who folded it and placed it over the back of the chair. Then he removed his shoes, socks, shirt, trousers, and undergarments. Now naked, the Leader turned to the mirror and looked closely at his own face.

"My makeup, Watson," he said, and sat down.

Watson lifted the case off the table, opened it, and displayed the contents to the Leader.

"Let's see," mused the Leader, "what kind of mood am I in?"

"Frisky," said Watson. "I'm told it's a full house tonight, sir. You may want to wear the red dress."

"The red one, you say?" said the Leader. "I think not, Watson. Tonight I want to wear all white. Bring me the white Charles Worth satin gown, the white toeless Rio Del Largo shoes, and my favorite feathery white boa."

"Like a virgin," said Watson, drolly.

"That's exactly how I feel tonight, Watson," the Leader said as he applied eyeliner and white dusting powder. Then he smeared on red lip grease. "Like a virgin—just with big ruby-red lips."

Watson stepped over to a closet door, opened it, and reached inside. He came out with a plaster human head holding a woman's long blond wig made of human hair styled into tight ringlets. Garfield lifted the wig off the head and placed it on his own, pulling at it and struggling for a few seconds to get it properly in place but finally mounting it correctly on his head. Then he looked into the mirror.

"There she is," he said with satisfaction. "There's my girl."

Wig in place, he stood up and turned toward Watson.

"My shoes, Watson."

From the closet, Watson drew out a pair of white, size thirteen, double-wide, six-inch button-up pumps. Garfield, still naked, sat back down on the chair and put them on, admiring how they looked against his smooth, hairless legs.

"Now, the dress," he said in a softer voice.

Watson opened the closet door wide enough to reveal the floor-length white organza dress with a bustle in the rear that hung there.

"Ah," said Garfield. "The Worth gown."

Watson took it off the hanger and then held it out in front of the Leader, who gently stepped into it. Watson pulled it up over the Leader's hips to his shoulders and buttoned it closed.

Watson stepped back, and Garfield turned around to look at himself in the almost-full-length mirror leaning against the far wall.

"Perfect," he said. "Madam G is ready to go."

James A. Garfield had seen more than his fair share of man's inhumanity against man during the Great War, having witnessed thousands die on the battlefield. He himself was lucky to have escaped with only minor physical injuries. Once during a military march, he became separated from his unit and lost in the thick forests of the southeast for weeks, living on berries and small dead animals. He never lost faith, though, that he would be found, and a month later, a group of indigenous people found him sleeping next to an oak tree in the middle of the day.

He came from a patriotic military family, and young Garfield was raised to believe in service to the nation and in fighting the Anarchists, who wanted to split the united continent of Nena right down the middle into two parts: the east, where most of the population lived, and the west, where most of the natural resources were buried in the ground.

Garfield was groomed from an early age for a life in the military. His mother was distant, unaffectionate, and cared little about what happened to her children. She spent most of her time in the company of her husband's male friends, who were more than happy to take care of her while her husband was away on military assignment. When he reached fifteen, Garfield left home for good and joined the military as a battlefield cadet. He soon learned the horrors of war firsthand.

The Great War was a civil conflict between the eastern and the western parts of the continent of Nena, the so-called breadbasket of the world. Income inequality had led to the rise of the Anarchists, a western group who believed they were providing all the resources but were not being fairly compensated because of an eminent domain law crafted by bankers and lawyers back east.

Declaring themselves cheated and therefore entitled to break the law, they began a rebellion against the continental government, based in Washington, DC.

At first their protests were peaceful, but when the Leader sent in troops to arrest the Anarchists, they soon turned ugly. These arrests incited the people of the west to cross the Big River that ran north to south and retaliate by murdering a town of easterners on the other shore and displaying the dead bodies of men, women, and children along the river. With emotions on both sides running hot, the first major battle took place when one hundred continental troops from the east planned to travel across the Big River to capture a camp of Anarchists on the western shore. It turned out that the eastern troops were young and inexperienced; for some, it was their first time in battle.

Their senior officers were just as inexperienced. When they were almost across the river, the Anarchists struck back, terrifying the eastern troops, who panicked. They ordered the boats to turn around and were quickly caught in the swift-running current and capsized. Young men swam for their lives, and almost all drowned that day.

A few survivors made it to the western shore, and they were taken to the Anarchist headquarters and tortured until they renounced their government. More atrocious incidents between the armies of the east and the west followed, including numerous bloody battles, kidnappings of civilians, and brutal punishments for those on the other side, until thousands lay dead and hundreds of thousands were wounded in what become one of the worst confrontations in the continent's history.

"Ladies and gentlemen!" said Leader James A. Garfield in his guise as Madam G as he walked out on the stage to the opening tune being tapped out on the piano keys. "Welcome to my late night show at the downstairs Capital Club. I hope you appreciate it, because Jonny and I put a lot of hard work into this song I'm about to sing for you. Isn't that right, Jonny?"

Applause.

"Right," said Jonny, a skinny, slick-haired man of twenty-five with bony fingers who sat hunched over on a bench in front of the keyboard. He wore a white satin jacket that almost matched Madam G's gown.

More applause erupted from the audience. People were packed into the small space. They were either seated at tables or standing at the bar, and there was very little space for the waiters to deliver the absinthe cocktails everyone was drinking. Madam G stood on a circular stage under a gaslit spot that reflected her long, white gown into the audience. Garfield covered his bare shoulders with a white-feathered boa and moved closer to the audience.

"You know, I want to acknowledge that you, my dear fans, make this journey so much more thrilling," said Madam G. "Why, imagine if I didn't have you. With no one out there, who would I sing to?"

"Madam," a young male voice called out from the audience. "Sing us a tune about love."

Applause.

"Love!" Madam G brushed this off with a roll of his eyes. "I've had my share of heartbreak. Would you like to hear about it?"

More applause.

The audience members consisted largely of DC's elder politicians, rich businessmen, healthy corset models, and celebrities of the day—including Miss Sarah Bernhardt, whose tiny frame was propped up on the bar surrounded by a multitude of good-looking young men, even though she herself was about seventy years old.

"I'd like to sing a song now about both love and heartbreak," said Madam G as Jonny played a few soft notes in the background. "It's by Joseph Philbrick Webster and Maud Irving and was published just a few years ago, in 1860. It's called 'I'll Twine 'mid the Ringlets,' and it goes something like this."

I'll sing, and I'll dance,
My laugh shall be gay,
I'll cease this wild weeping
Drive sorrow away,
Tho' my heart is now breaking,
He never shall know,
That his name made me tremble
And my pale cheek to glow.

CHAPTER NINE

The ghost of Juanita Redmond, Leader Garfield's mother-in-law who was strangled by Doc Holliday in the park, surprised the cook one morning by dismantling the pantry and destroying all the dry goods. But that was not the first ghost sighting in the house. Late at night, with more recurring frequency, Juanita's poltergeist would walk the long, silent hallways of Garfield's stately home in Washington, DC, often breaking mirrors and defacing family portraits with animal blood and feces. The last straw came one day when the ghost lifted her twin grandsons out of their cribs and carried them outside the home unnoticed. They were found the next day lying unharmed on the damp grass in the front yard.

Emotionally unable to cope, Lucretia Garfield, who was traumatized by her dead mother's return, asked a mystic doctor friend for advice.

Dr. Adrian Warlock was the flamboyant founding member of Witchluxe, an international society of paranormal investigators who policed otherworldly crimes committed by gruesome ghouls, mischievous monsters, vicious vampyrs, wicked witches, dangerous demons, and other abusers of the dark arts.

"You say the ghost visits you often," said Dr. Warlock. "How often?"

"Almost every day," said Lucretia. "We're worried about the boys. The ghost, or whatever it was, carried them outside last week, and we're lucky to have them back."

"Yes," said Dr. Warlock, "it sounds like this could be a malicious spirit looking for revenge."

"Revenge?" asked Lucretia. "Against whom?"

"Why, her killer, of course," said Dr. Warlock. "I'll bet being murdered really pissed her off."

"What do you recommend, Doctor?" she asked. "I'm at wit's end."

"A séance," Dr. Warlock said. "Performed at the stroke of midnight."

At eleven thirty that night, on a foggy, gaslit street in Washington, DC, Dr. Warlock stepped out of a horse-drawn carriage to the pavement in front of the Leader Garfield's home. The dashing witch, who looked about thirty years of age, wore a long, dark-gray woolen cape with red silk lining over a three-piece, charcoal-gray pinstriped suit, black leather shoes with clean soles, and a green felt fedora hat. His long brown hair was tied back in a ponytail. His face was long and narrow, but his eyes were warm and curious. Thin lips and a small mustache sat under a prominent nose.

Dr. Warlock's familiar, his witch compatriot, was a silver-tipped walking stick named Maxine that he always carried with him, and he used it now to knock on Garfield's door.

After about a minute, the door opened, and the housekeeper admitted him and led him through a richly decorated hallway, where precious antiques, statuary, and giant potted palms were displayed in abundance. He followed the housekeeper down the hallway, stepping carefully over the expensive carpets, until they stopped in front of a set of closed ornately-carved doors, beyond which he could sense a lingering spirit lying in wait.

"Well, Maxine?" Dr. Warlock said to his walking stick. "Can you feel it—the hostility coming from inside the room?"

"I beg your pardon, sir?" said the housekeeper as she opened the doors and pointed the way in.

"Yeah, Doc," Maxine said. "It feels cold, as if we're walking into a grave."

Inside the parlor, harsh electric lighting revealed a fussy interior framed by stuffy portraits, shelves boasting an inordinate number of books, and delicate brocade furniture that looked too fragile to be used. A large stone fireplace sat at the south end of the room, and in front of it stood a large circular games table surrounded by four chairs.

"This house is haunted by two spirits," said Dr. Warlock, entering the room. "An old woman who can't find her way out...and a demon that won't let her go."

"Yes, sir," said the housekeeper as she disappeared, closing the doors behind her.

"I can feel them," Maxine said. "And they know we're here."

Dr. Warlock moved slowly around the room, waving Maxine in the air as if she could breathe magic. He stopped before an oil-painted portrait of Leader Garfield above the mantle of the stone fireplace.

"Dr. Adrian Warlock, I presume?"

Garfield himself had appeared out of a dark corner of the room, entering through a secret door without making a sound. He extended his hand. Another man stood behind him but was barely visible in the darkness.

"Leader, it is a pleasure to meet you," Dr. Warlock said, shaking hands.

"Please, call me James," the Leader said. "I wish we'd met under less stressful circumstances."

"Doc is the one under stress," said Maxine. "To perform."

"Perform?" asked Garfield.

"Get rid of your ghosts," said Maxine. "You have two."

"I've sent Lucretia and the boys away for the night," said Garfield, "as I expect this could get ugly."

"Like Doc's temper," said Maxine, who had a wry sense of humor.

"Be quiet, Maxine," said Dr. Warlock. "Let us see where this ghost hunt takes us."

"Oh," said Garfield, "I'd like to introduce my new bodyguard. This is Stig."

Stig, standing a muscular six feet, five inches tall, stepped out of the shadows. He was met by Dr. Warlock's walking stick.

"Would you mind holding Maxine for me, Stig?" Dr. Warlock asked. "I'm taking your temperature—paranormally speaking, of course."

"Uh...yeah. OK."

Stig took hold of the cherrywood walking stick. Its silver-topped handle was shaped like the head of a falcon and had two inlaid rubies for eyes that when in danger blinked bright red. In ancient times, it had belonged to pharaohs. Having then passed into the possession of witches, it now belonged to Dr. Warlock.

"Hold me tighter, Stig," said Maxine, demurely. "I won't break."

"I sense from my psychic examination, young man," said Dr. Warlock, "that you're afraid of ghosts and really do not want to be here."

"That's a little harsh, Adrian," said Garfield, "don't you think?"

"Not afraid," Stig replied, handing the walking stick back. "Anxious."

"I'm sure you're not being honest with yourself," said the doctor of spells and incantations. "But one does need four people to conduct a séance."

"Ah, yes, this séance?" Garfield said. "I'm not sure I agree."

"It's the only way to be rid of ghosts, James," said Dr. Warlock. "My familiar here, Maxine, happens to be my spirit guide and will steer us through the séance and rid you of those pesky ghosts."

"Maxine?" Garfield asked. "Humm."

"What ya looking at, Your Highness?" asked Maxine, annoyed.

"Nothing. I—"

"Good," she said. "We have ghosts to scare off."

"James," asked Dr. Warlock, "can we shut off those glaring overhead lights?"

"Yes, certainly." Garfield stepped over to a switch on the wall and turned them off. The room fell into darkness. Without saying a word, Stig lit a kerosene lamp and placed it in the middle of the games table.

"Very good, Stig," said Dr. Warlock. "You followed my mental instructions exactly."

"You mean...you're using your mind to nonverbally communicate with Stig?" asked Garfield.

"More like magically communicate," Dr. Warlock said. "Stig is quite susceptible to certain paranormal activity and could easily be manipulated by spirits that reside inside this room, so I've put him into a mild trance—nothing that will cause him any permanent harm. He will respond to you like normal."

"And I gave him a mild sedative when he touched me," said Maxine, "to assist Dr. Warlock's spell."

"Yes, Maxine," said Dr. Warlock. "Thank you for your assistance. I couldn't have done it without you."

Suddenly, the magic walking stick flew out of Dr. Warlock's hand and landed upright on the parlor floor in front of the games table, where it glowed red and emitted light-gray smoke that momentarily filled the room before disappearing up the fireplace chimney. In place of the smoke stood a young, statuesque redheaded woman wearing a long, deep-red satin gown and black gloves that rose to her elbows.

"How dramatic, Maxine," said Dr. Warlock. "But we're wasting time."

"Relax, Doctor," she said. "I've only taken this form because you need a fourth for the séance. Unless someone wants to hold my stick?"

"Tone it down, Maxine," said Dr. Warlock. "Now, James, if you and Stig would take your seats around the games table, we can begin."

"What about me?" Maxine asked. "Where do I go?"

"Such a loaded question," Dr. Warlock said with a smirk. "Just sit anywhere you like, Maxine. Thanks."

All three sat down at the table, the kerosene lamp in the middle the only source of light in the room. Dr. Warlock looked around, took off his long woolen cape, and laid it over a parlor chair.

"Before I join you at the table," he said, "I want you to understand what's about to happen so that you'll be prepared for the worst."

"What?" Garfield asked.

"The worst," said Maxine.

The kerosene lamp's flame began to flicker, casting strange shadows on the silk-papered walls.

"James," Dr. Warlock said, "your mother-in-law's ghost has somehow been taken over by a demon, and my job is to drive it out of her using a cleansing spell of bright-white light. Do not be afraid when the whole room fills up with the light. Maxine will guide Juanita's spirit from this world and on to the next. Do either of you have any questions?"

Stig looked blankly into space.

Maxine fussed with her bright-red hair.

Garfield look petrified.

"I might add," Dr. Warlock said, "that what will happen next is very dangerous, and any one of us, except possibly Maxine—but that's another story—could be killed."

"As long as my family is safe," said Garfield. "My life is expendable."

"Hold that thought," said Maxine. "It just might happen."

Dr. Warlock threw Maxine a wilting look before taking his seat at the table.

"Please join hands," he said. "The séance is about to begin."

CHAPTER TEN

"Spirits, hear me!" Dr. Warlock called out as he sat with the others at the circular games table in the near-dark parlor room of Leader Garfield's home. "I'm calling on Juanita Redmond, Lucretia Garfield's mother, to appear before us and explain your actions."

"I'm not sure I believe, in ghosts" said Garfield. "I mean, strange things have occurred in this house, but—"

"Quiet!" said Maxine, who tightened her grip on his hand. "The maestro is at work."

The kerosene lamp on the table moved by itself a few inches toward Garfield.

"I know someone is here," said Dr. Warlock. "Tell us, spirit, are you Juanita?"

After a few moments, chains rattled, and a woman's scream turned into a gurgled yelp.

"Was that her?" asked Garfield. "Juanita, are you here with us?"

"Wherrrre...izz...my...brain?" came a deep voice from the darkness near the mantel.

"This is not Juanita," warned Dr. Warlock. "It is the demon itself."

Bam! The heavy wooden parlor doors both blew open.

Rattle, rattle. The glass panes in the front windows began to vibrate and shake, until finally the one on the end exploded into the parlor in a fury of wind and flying glass.

"Darn! Who's going to clean that up?" asked Garfield. "I gave the housekeeper the rest of the night off."

"I'll take care of it," said Maxine, starting to get up to take a closer look.

"Sit down, Maxine," said Dr. Warlock. He looked to his right. Stig got up, walked toward the broken window, turned back, and looked around the room.

"That's right—the table."

Stig grabbed a heavy coffee table, lifted it as if it were paper, and then propped it against the broken window to block the night's draft. *Swoosh!* A gust of wind blew into the room from the open fireplace chimney with such violence that the stuffy portraits were knocked off the wall.

"Mischievous demon, show yourself!" Dr. Warlock commanded.

The wind in the room picked up, making it difficult for Stig to get back to his seat, as if trying to prevent him from rejoining the séance.

"Doctor," asked Maxine, "where is it hiding?"

"It's moving around the room," he said. "Right now, it's standing between James and Stig."

Leader Garfield turned his head to the right, but no one was there. Maxine looked at him and smiled.

"It's a strange business, this paranormal life," said Maxine. "Not for the faint of heart."

"Wherrrre…izzzz…my…brain?" came out of Stig's mouth. He was still in Dr. Warlock's trance.

"What's he mumbling?" asked Garfield.

"Brains, Leader," said Maxine. "They always want brains."

"I smell smoke!" Garfield said and stood up in alarm as the parlor drapes, rugs, and furniture burst into flames, surrounding the circular games table in a ring of fire.

Maxine, who was deathly afraid of fire, jumped up from the table and screamed, beginning to tear at her own facial skin in fear. Panicked, she looked around for a place to run, but the flames were everywhere. Garfield, however, had the opposite reaction—he seemed to be fascinated by the flames, at one point picking up a flaming book that had fallen on the floor.

Finally, Dr. Warlock stood up, grabbed Maxine, and shook her.

"It's a trick!" he shouted over the roaring fire. "The demon wants us to falter and fail."

"Help me, Doc!" Maxine begged. "I'm losing my control."

"Evernmentum, braxous!" Dr. Warlock spoke in the language of the Ancients.

The winds stopped, the flames were sucked up into the chimney and out of the room, and everything fell back into its usual place.

"James?" asked Dr. Warlock, still holding a shaken Maxine.

"I'm fine," said Garfield, sitting back down. "Let's continue."

"Magic can be addictive," said Maxine, now too resuming her seat at the table, "if you let it get the best of you."

"Right," said Garfield. "Adrian, what's wrong with Stig? He hasn't said a word in hours—except those of the demon."

"He's fine," said Dr. Warlock. "If he weren't under my coercion spell, he would be susceptible to ghostly invasion."

"Let's rejoin our hands," said Maxine.

"Hear me, demon!" Dr. Warlock said loudly as his body began to glow in a white light that suddenly illuminated everyone at the table. "Show yourself now, or face the full power of Stonehenge."

"Nottt...'frraid...yoouu...warlock," the voice in the dark said. "Youu...will allll...diiiie."

"It's gotten cold in here," said Garfield.

"Can you feel it, Doc?" asked Maxine. "That dread of feeling completely alone?"

"Yes, I do, Maxine," he said. "This demon is powerful, playing games with our emotions. We need to stand strong against it, or all may be lost."

The kerosene lamp in the middle of the table started to shake, nearly extinguishing the only light in the room, as if something wanted them left in the dark.

"I don't think you're getting through to it, Adrian," said Garfield.

"Doc knows what he's doing," said Maxine.

"The vile beast is standing right behind you, James," said Dr. Warlock. "Please don't move. It's reaching out to touch you."

"Don't move?" asked Garfield, beginning to panic. "Tell that to my bowels."

"You...tempt...meee," said the unseen demon, "to crussssshhh youu...like a bug."

"Release this man and his mother-in-law from your evil grasp, demon!" shouted Dr. Warlock. "I command you!"

"Never," it said. "She is mine, as *he* will be, forever."

The kerosene lamp flew off the table and crashed to the floor, bursting into flames.

"Ha ha ha!" laughed the demon, who now began to materialize in the flames, revealing a fish-scaly face, piercing red eyes, sharp claws touching Garfield's shoulder, cloven feet under what appeared to be a seven-foot serpent-like body—and a bad attitude.

"Braxous, mercalous!" shouted Dr. Warlock with a wave of his hand, and the burning fire blew out at his command, leaving the room in complete darkness. The demon was nowhere to be seen.

Garfield tried to stand up, but Stig grabbed his arm and pulled him back down into his seat.

"James," a frail, raspy voice called out in the dark. "Help me."

"Juanita?" asked Garfield. "Is that you?"

"I'll bet not," said Maxine. "Doc, we need some light here."

Dr. Warlock snapped his fingers, and blue flames appeared on his fingertips. The light illuminated Juanita's spirit, disheveled and dripping wet, standing next to the seated Garfield.

"Time to join her," said the demon, speaking through Stig.

He grabbed Garfield by the throat and pulled him out of his chair. Maxine tried to intervene, but Juanita's spirit restrained her. Magically, they both disappeared, and only Maxine materialized at the opposite end of the room.

Stig was crushing Garfield's windpipe.

"I've lost control over Stig," said Dr. Warlock. "The demon has him!"

"Do something!" shouted Maxine, whose feet seemed to be buried up to her ankles in the wooden floor. She was unable to move.

"Abracadalious, pertaninum," Dr. Warlock said, and a blue flame ignited in the palm of his hand.

He blew on the flame and it leaped right into Stig's face and then covered the rest of his body. Stig released Garfield, who was magically not touched by the flames, and then ran screaming in circles around the room before jumping through one of the parlor windows and landing outside, his dead body aflame on the sidewalk and casting bright light into the darkness.

"I guess you'll be looking for a new bodyguard?" Maxine asked from across the room.

"Very funny, Maxine," said Dr. Warlock. "Things often don't turn out as we plan."

"How about a little help?" she said. "And a little less lecturing."

"Omonorris, beganta," said Dr. Warlock, and Maxine stepped up out of the entrapping floor, walked back across the room, and resumed her seat.

"Thanks."

The parlor was now in complete darkness except for the light coming in from the street through the broken windows, revealing smashed furniture and singed draperies flung all over the room.

"James, please be seated," Dr. Warlock said. "We need to finish this."

"I don't think it's been going too well so far, Adrian," said Garfield. "Do you?"

"Hold my hand, dearie," Maxine said. "I'll protect you."

They joined hands.

"You said we need four people to do the séance," said Garfield.

"In a pinch," said Dr. Warlock, who closed his eyes to concentrate.

"Doctor," Maxine said, "something's standing right behind you."

The "thing" exhibited the same fish-scaly skin as the last one, but this was definitely a different demon—it had big horns sprouting from its forehead, and very sharp snapping teeth that it displayed without provocation.

"Warlock diiies...now!" the demon said in a groan. It reached out to grab Dr. Warlock by the neck, but its hands passed right through without touching solid flesh.

"Adrian?" asked Garfield, nervously.

"I'm over here," said Dr. Warlock, who stood by the mantel. "That was my astral self. Everyone who works for Witchluxe has one."

The demon charged the table, reaching for Garfield. With only a few seconds to spare, Dr. Warlock appeared next to Maxine, who returned to her walking stick form. He picked her up off her chair, waved her in the air, and gave the demon a powerful shock. It retaliated by knocking Maxine out of the warlock's hand and cutting him deep with its claws.

"Doc, it's time to end this," said Maxine from the floor.

"Trying, Maxine," he said. "*Omonorris, beganta!*"

The astral self escaped Dr. Warlock's body a second time, floated through the air, and wrapped itself tightly around the demon's body, rendering it unable to move. It struggled fiercely, but the astral self did not relent until it and the demon literally disappeared into the void.

"What's going on here?" cried Garfield.

"He's squeezed the demon back from whence it came," said Maxine.

"But," said Garfield, "what happened to my mother-in-law?"

"Here...James," came a raspy female voice. "Come...find me."

Half-hidden in a dark corner of the room, visible in the street light, stood an old, gray-haired woman, maybe four feet tall and dressed all in gray, wearing a shawl that almost covered her face and her dull, dead eyes.

"Madam," said Dr. Warlock, "it's time for you to go, and with help from my spirit guide, Maxine, we will send you on your way."

"Be...ware," it said. "Holl-o-way..."

"Time to go, Grandma," said Maxine, opening the portal between the living and dead.

"Holloway?" said Dr. Warlock, whose hand wound had completely healed. "I don't recognize the name."

"I do," said Garfield. "But the name isn't Holloway. It's *Holliday*, and my dead mother-in-law didn't come back from the grave to haunt us, but to warn us about the man who may have killed her—Doc Holliday."

CHAPTER ELEVEN

Inventor Alex G. Bell stood inside a dark tunnel, and he was terrified. He'd been afraid of everything since he was a very young child and had to force himself to interact with people and not run and hide. Suddenly he saw orbs of light coming toward him, and then he saw the approaching dead gold miners, their bodies hunched over, their flesh rotting off their bones, walking in a procession out of the tunnel and into the moonlight. They wore torn overalls covered in dirt and mud, black high-top boots, and dented metal hats, and all carried round lanterns.

"Hello?" Bell called out. "It's so quiet in this place I was beginning to worry if anyone was here."

The skeletal gold miners—who had perished underground years ago during a cave-in caused by an explosion on the surface—approached the spot where he stood but did not appear to see him.

"I'm lost, you see," he said. "Not sure how I got here. Do you know the way out?"

To his astonishment, the thirty-five lost gold miners all passed right through him and continued on, descending back into the darkness and taking their lantern light with them.

He was again alone in the dark.

Drip, drip.

Dripping water.

Rumble.

Then the ground underneath him shook, and he heard cracking timber, which preceded the roof's caving in on top of him. Bell was pinned to the cavern floor, lying on his back and barely breathing. Panic set in. He could feel the weight of the dirt and timber on his chest, and normal breathing was almost impossible. As he gasped for air, dirt entered his mouth. It tasted terrible—all wet and sandy, with small stones mixed in that could potentially block his windpipe, making it even harder for him to breathe. Then he heard a faint sound, like something clawing or scratching as it moved closer to him.

Maybe someone is coming to rescue me, Bell thought. But his hope soon turned to fear when the sound became more savage. It frightened him so much that he wanted to scream, but when he opened his mouth, he only swallowed more dirt. The scratching sound grew louder, and a shrill, high-pitched sound heralded the appearance of a strange-looking mammal that burst through the dirt next to his head. Using its slimy tongue, it licked off clumps of his hair and began to nibble on his earlobe with its scalpel-sharp teeth. Bell felt warm blood trickle down to the base of his neck as the translucent, almost milky-white weasel-sized creature with six legs finished off his ear and started to bite the skin around his skull while making sucking sounds that grew more active as it fed.

Tears rolled down Bell's cheeks as he struggled to free himself from under the heavy weight, but he could not move an inch in either direction. The horrible creature finally managed to chew a hole through his head and then squeezed its way into the skull cavity, biting down on his brain with such ferocious force that it popped open and splattered blood everywhere in his dream.

Bell, a short, average-looking man in his midtwenties with a mustache and spectacles, had been suffering from horrific nightmares almost every night since he'd arrived in Ghost Town. He'd come by stagecoach at the insistence of Doc Holliday as a way to pay off his debt and now feared for his life.

Being born to a wealthy family had allowed Bell the luxury of learning everything he wanted about science, particularly the study of magnetic energy, without ever having to pay for college himself, and it had allowed him time to pursue his lifelong goal of discovering new and renewable energy sources to save the environment from the human race. The only thing that stood in Bell's way was his misanthropy, and he had no personal life. He was bored with people most of the time and preferred his studies to social interaction. If not home alone, Bell spent his time in the campus library, hiding up in the corner and looking through old patents and earthquake maps for evidence of large electromagnetic wave events. Graduating with honors, he was quickly recruited by the Crosslands Railroad and sent out west, where he worked as a timekeeper, making sure the trains ran on time and visiting areas in his territory that needed either improvement or expansion.

"We want you to start from the ground up," said the boss. "Once you know everything about our railroad, we'll ask you to design a plan to change it for the better."

Bored after only a few weeks, Bell soon realized his future was not in timekeeping but in the copper wire that was strung and nailed to eleven-foot wooden poles along the railroad tracks. Working nights when everyone else was asleep, he experimented with the flow of electromagnetic energy using a conductor of copper wire to create a small, square box that could regulate and direct the flow of energy into a new type of code—impulses turned into letters and then words into sentences. Within two months, a new messaging language was born, which Bell named "telewire."

When the higher-ups at the railroad heard of Bell's new invention, they sensed an opportunity to profit greatly and filed a patent for the new code. They put Bell in charge of the whole operation and doubled his resources—more staff, unlimited access, and a better place to live—because they believed a fortune could be made from charging people willing to pay for the privilege of communicating over long distances without the need to travel.

With the added resources Bell was able to prove out his telewire as it soon became apparent that people were addicted to this new form of communication, especially those in love.

"I'd like to commend Alex Bell," telewired Leader Garfield in his first continental communication to the people of Nena Continent, "on his invention of the life-changing new language that I use today."

The telewire opened up the west like never before. For the first time, merchants in the east who agreed to subsidize the telewire build-out could transact directly with buyers in the west. Regulations out of Washington, DC, were relaxed, and the trading of goods and services drove the economy higher. This new boom also coincided with the new fiscal and immigration policies of Leader Garfield, whose liberal social beliefs and conservative economics combined to pull the Nena Continent out of recession and back to full production, opening up the west for exploration while building a social safety net for all with the profits. He pioneered universal income for all and subsidized housing for anyone who requested it, encouraging many dense eastern city dwellers to move south and west for a better life with guaranteed income and housing.

The Leader's popularity was at a record high as he planned a trip across the country "to meet his people." But not everyone was rooting for the Leader to succeed. The old guard—the regional overlords, political appointees, and old wealth—wanted to keep their power, and it wasn't long before savage fighting broke out between government troops and local homegrown militias backed by his enemies.

"Extra! Extra!" the telewire tapped out. "Leader Garfield calls out the troops. The western bloc said not to concede even after hundreds dead and dying."

Garfield stood tall and never regretted his action, realizing that a united continent was the only way that everyone would share equally in this new communications revolution created by Alex Bell, a man who had little use for the rest of society.

Boom!

A second *boom!*

The mountains west of Ghost Town shook, rumbled, and released tons of dirt and rock into the air and down into the valley. Miles away, at the north end of town, Alex G. Bell held the device that had detonated both bombs remotely.

"Congratulations," said Doc Holliday, who had arrived on horseback unannounced. "Now, where is *my* bomb?"

Bell jumped, caught completely by surprise.

"You scared the life out of me!" he said, gasping to catch his breath.

"You're jumpy today, Bell," said Holliday. "I told ya, ghosts only come out at night. Ha ha ha! Now, tell me what you're doing."

"I'm testing the detonation device," Bell said. "Each time a little farther away."

"And?"

"And," said Bell, "the long-distance detonation was a success."

"Good. Now, when can I have my bomb?"

"I've got to build a new bomb," Bell said. "Then you can have it."

"How long?"

"A week."

"Nope," said Holliday. "A day—or you're dead."

"That's impossible. I've run out of gunpowder. It will take at least a couple of days to get more."

"Nonsense. You'll have it tomorrow."

"If you're in such a hurry," said Bell, "why don't you build it yourself?"

"I have more important things to attend to, Bell. Just build my bomb."

"I don't like it here. Have you seen the woman who walks around in a dress holding her own head?"

"That's Miss Jenkins," Holliday said. "She used to be my nanny when I was very small."

"I'll bet," said Bell. "Did you have anything to do with the head?"

"A small child?" asked Holliday. "How could I possibly…" He trailed off.

"Yes?"

"As a matter of fact," Holliday said, "I'm the one who cut off her head, with the cook's knife. Daddy was so pissed for weeks, until we got a new cook."

Building out the telewire network across the continent had almost exhausted Bell. The endless stress caused by delays, the long nights that ran into dawn, and the pushy higher-ups in the railroad who wanted it done all took their toll, and mistakes were made, providing the railroad with an excuse to get rid of him. He was fired from the network he'd created for incompetence and sent back east, where he quickly went through his savings gambling and carousing. He was disowned by his family and became almost destitute. Then, one night in a local saloon in Washington, DC, he met Doc Holliday, who was traveling and offered to fund Bell's dreams and in turn force him to invent a way to detonate a bomb from a long distance away.

"Stop whining," said Holliday, "and finish building my bomb. You owe me, and I own you now, and until you pay me back, you'll have to do whatever I ask."

Bell's inability to pay his debt was the reason he'd agreed to move west to work for Holliday. Since the day he'd arrived in Ghost Town, he had constantly feared for his life. To him the town seemed a very strange place. It was dead quiet almost all the time and run down to the point of being decrepit, and very few residents ventured outside at night. He himself had seen strange apparitions, and he'd heard cries of babies that never could be found. Realizing he was stuck, Bell decided he would make the best of his situation and use this forced opportunity to do his own research on electromagnetic waves.

"I know what I owe you, Holliday," said Bell. "But why do you want such a powerful bomb...and one that can be detonated from a long distance?"

"That's none of your concern," said Holliday, curtly. "You're to build what I ask without questioning my motives."

"I'd rather not hurt anyone," said Bell. "It goes against my nature."

Holliday dismounted his horse and walked over to Bell.

"OK, Bell," said Holliday, pulling his gun from a hidden waist holster, pointing it at Bell's head, and cocking it. "Let me make this perfectly clear. If you cross me once or fail to do what I ask you without hesitation...well, I'm afraid I'll have no choice but to blow your brains out."

CHAPTER TWELVE

Back in town, in the sheriff's office, Nikki Hale and Annie Oakley were sitting quietly at the desk, each somewhat lost in her own thoughts, when the door flew open and sunshine filled the room.

"I'm sorry to keep you ladies waiting," said Sheriff Wyatt Earp as he removed his hat. Rhino Bill Cody followed him in. "But there's a lot going on today, what with the explosions and all."

"No need to apologize, Sheriff," said Nikki. "Annie and I were just having a great discussion about her future."

"We was?" Annie asked, blushing. "I don't remember that."

Rhino Bill took off his hat and leaned against the back wall.

"Well, Miss," said Earp, "I'd like to talk to you about leaving Ghost Town as a precaution...and as soon as possible."

Nikki, taken aback, rose from her seat and faced the much taller Earp.

"Sheriff, where would I go?" she asked. "I'm not from around here."

"It's not safe here for you," said Earp. "There may be trouble."

"Trouble?" she asked.

"Why, Sheriff," said Annie, "I do believe you care."

"Hush, Annie."

"I can help, Sheriff," said Nikki. "I have experience."

"Uh...what do you do, exactly?" asked Earp.

"In the future, I'm a crime fighter," Nikki said. "I'm expert at hand-to-hand combat, high-wire acrobatics, and camouflaged surveillance."

"I think staying here is a really bad idea, Miss," said Earp.

"Please," she said, "stop calling me Miss. My name is Nikki."

"Nikki," he said. "I'm just concerned for your safety."

"Please, Sheriff," said Nikki, looking directly into his soft, twinkling brown eyes. "Annie told me about your wife, and...I can protect myself. I want to stay here in Ghost Town until I can figure out how to get back to my own time."

"Bill?" asked Earp. "What do you think?"

"I think she looks like she can handle herself," he said.

"Annie?"

"We do need extra hands," said Annie. "You said so yourself."

"I wouldn't be any trouble," said Nikki.

"Where would you stay?" Earp asked.

"I was hoping I could stay at your house for the time being," she said. "If it's no trouble."

Rhino Bill and Annie exchanged glances.

"Well..." Sheriff Earp said. "I..."

"Quiet as a little mouse," said Nikki, smiling as she feigned buttoning her lips. "I promise."

"OK," the sheriff said. "Nikki, you can stay with me for now, but only until we figure out a longer-term solution."

"Wow, thanks, Sheriff!" she said.

"Ah." He blushed. "You can call me Wyatt."

Thirteen-year-old Nikki Hale lay on her back in the gutter, felled by a gunshot wound to her head. Still alive, she watched a pigeon fly above her from one fire escape to another as her own blood washed into the sewer and disappeared under the ground. The street was empty of people and hovertraffic; it was so quiet she could hear a dog barking somewhere off in the distance. Then it faded away, as did she, moving in and out of consciousness. When a robotic hovercraft drove by to wash down the street, she woke up but was unable to move, and it didn't stop to help her. She did not feel the cool water it sprayed, because her body was dying, numbed by the pain.

The illegal weapon that had been used to shoot her was lying on the curb, covered in Nikki's splattered blood. The man who had shot her, a small-time local pimp named Fredor, had dropped it when he'd run away from the scene of his heinous crime. He was furious that Nikki had interfered with one of his girls whom he liked to beat up—he felt she had no business interfering in his stuff. Though a thief, Nikki had never been sold for sex and often tried to get the other girls on her block to avoid Fredor and his vile business. Unfortunately, most of the girls who rebelled against him would end up beaten, dead, or lost to dope.

"I told you to stay away from my girl," Fredor had said earlier that day.

"She's not your property, Freddie," Nikki yelled back. "None of them are."

"You got in my business," he said, pulling a small handgun out of his waistband. "Now I'm gonna put you out of the way."

Street-trained from an early age to defend herself, Nikki swift-kicked the gun out of Fredor's hand and used her clenched fist to punch him in the jaw.

"Ouch, girl!" said Fredor. "That hurt!"

"Leave those girls alone, Freddie," she said, "and get a real job."

"Or else what?" he asked, holding his sore jaw. "You can't stop me. You're just a little girl."

Nikki charged, delivering quite a few more blows that almost had Fredor on the ground, but he was over six feet tall and weighed two hundred pounds. Much smaller and lighter, Nikki found it very hard to take him down.

"Tiring out, little thief?" he joked, managing to send a punch to her chest that knocked Nikki into the street, where she tripped over the curb and fell. He ran and picked up the gun, a self-made weapon he'd learned how to build on the Net, and then turned, aimed, and fired as Nikki began to stand up in the gutter. The bullet ripped through her lung, which quickly filled up with blood, forcing her to gasp for breath. Fredor shot again, this time hitting Nikki in the forehead, forcing her back down. He dropped the gun and ran way as Nikki lay dying in the gutter with no one around to help—pretty much how she had spent the first thirteen years of her life.

Abandoned in a basket on an empty street as a newborn by a philandering father and an opium-addicted mother, Nikki had been found and named by the orphanage where she grew up in Casino City, the capital of Atlantica Continent and a place known for its wild nightlife, multiple forms of gambling, seven-star food, and legalized prostitution. The pleasure continent of Atlantica was a vacation paradise and, for some, a never-ending nightmare. Even the orphanage gambled with government money meant to care for the young, using it instead to play blackjack.

Nikki learned how to survive as soon as she could walk. Gifted with the power of common sense, she learned by observing other people, usually successful people with wealth she'd seen in and around the casinos. With help of Kat, an older ex-boxer who lived across the street from the orphanage in an SRO flophouse, she also learned how to defend herself after being molested twice by doctors at the orphanage.

Kat taught her how to fight with her whole body—feet, fists, and forehead. Working out daily from the age of five, Nikki grew stronger and street smarter every day. She stole what she needed on the outside to survive and had no problem with it, for it was the only life she knew. When the orphanage gambled and lost the monthly expense fund, there would be no food, so she had to steal to feed herself and the others she had befriended there.

Around the age of ten, Nikki finally escaped the orphanage for good and began to steal larger items—hovercraft, jewelry, art—always using her talent to blend in and go about unnoticed. After securing a place to live in the arcade area not far from the orphanage, she set about helping others and using her ill-gotten gains to feed both young and old in the neighborhood—and fighting for them if the need arose.

Physically, she was ready for the job. Through her training with Kat, Nikki excelled at gymnastics, climbing, running, and fistfighting, showing no fear. Her young body was hard and lean, and she could outrun anyone, including the police in her neighborhood. Eventually, she became known as Red Ghost, a local hero, because she always wore dark red clothing and could disappear into the woodwork to spy and infiltrate what she considered prime targets.

Trying to keep herself afloat financially, Nikki rolled drunken gamblers by hiding in hotel hallways, picked pockets of rich patrons on crowded casino floors, and shoplifted expensive clothing from boutiques on the beach, which she always gave away to the poor who lived on the streets near the orphanage. Despite her age and size, Nikki's reputation for doing good spread, and Red Ghost was cheered and feared on the street, either way keeping the aggressive adults from hurting her friends at the orphanage.

But that all changed when Fredor, the charming pimp, moved into the neighborhood. Humpy and rough, he hung around the block every day and watched all the young children coming and going from the orphanage. Little by little, he befriended some of them and persuaded them to do favors for men who paid. When Nikki found out he was targeting underage kids to pimp out, she confronted him, but he would not stop. She never gave up, though, and over the years she was able to save many children—until that one fateful day when she confronted him on the street.

"And he put a bullet through my head, and I died."

"Only I didn't stay dead for long," Nikki said. "The pimp's bullet pierced my skull, and as I lay dying in the street, a strange thing happened. I sat up and stepped out of my own body. When I looked down, there I was, still in the gutter, lying motionless with my blood leaking down the sewer. I got a very strange feeling, and I looked at my hands—they were transparent. I could see right through them. I wasn't quite sure what had happened to me or why I'd return as a ghost, but that was my reality."

"So," said Rhino Bill, "you died and came back from the dead?"

"No, I was still dead," said Nikki, "but my life force hadn't given up, or something. I never found out the real reason why. I just knew that my body had died, and I had become transparent, and I could move through anything—including walls, floors, even people—with just a thought. It was all very unsettling at the time, like learning to walk all over again."

"What did your friends at the orphanage do?" asked Annie.

"Everyone ran away from me," Nikki said. "Terrified."

"Well, I guess I can see that," said Earp. "You being a ghost and all."

"In death I'd been given another surprise," she said. "I was able to step inside people and short-circuit their brains with an electrical impulse. Again, I'm not sure where it came from, but that's what I can do. So, when I caught up with Fredor, I walked inside of him and zapped him long enough for the authorities, whom I had alerted, to arrive, and he was put away for life."

"That's quite a tale, Nikki," said Earp. "So, let me see if I've got this right. In the future, you died as a teen, and somehow you traveled back in time to Ghost Town, where now you're a living, breathing adult."

"Crazy, right?" she said.

"I'll say," said Rhino Bill. "But I seen a lot of strange things in this world, so why not a teen ghost turned, ah…"

"Into a lady," said Annie.

"It gets even stranger," said Nikki. "Sheriff—I mean Wyatt—you were there with me in the future. At least, an older version of you, and you saved my life by bringing me here at the moment Grimm was about to lower his blade."

"It's fate," said Annie. "She came here to help us."

"I think that remains to be seen, Annie," said Earp.

"Wyatt, when you first found me naked outside of town," Nikki said, "I didn't remember any of this, but it started to come back to me over time, and now I know who I am and how I got here—you brought me."

"You say we worked together in the future," said Earp. "I don't remember you."

"We fought side by side as Protectors," Nikki said.

"Protectors?" said Rhino Bill. "What are they?"

"A group of gifted and specially trained heroes," said Nikki. "More like family, they came together during periods of great violence and criminality, vowing to protect mankind from any and all threats. Their history actually goes way back to ancient times."

"And you say I was one of them?" asked Earp. "The Protectors?"

"Yes," said Nikki. "You were a valuable member of the team—a pathfinder…and the man who saved my life."

"Shucks," said Annie. "You two was meant to be together."

"Seems that way to me," Rhino Bill agreed.

"If there's trouble brewing," said Nikki. "Maybe we should form our own team, and we could call ourselves the new Protectors."

Nikki and the sheriff stood side by side on the front porch of the jail, watching as Annie and Rhino Bill mounted their horses.

"We'll see you tomorrow after dawn," said Annie. She turned to Rhino Bill. "I promised Nikki I'd let her shoot my gun for practice and that we'd get her a horse."

"Yes, dear," said Rhino Bill, and off they rode down Main Street toward their camp outside town.

"I hope my staying with you is OK," said Nikki. "I realize Annie was pressuring you a bit."

"No, it's fine," said Earp with a smile. "Actually, I'd appreciate the company. It gets very lonely…" He paused, perhaps thinking about his wife, Katie, still missing and presumed dead.

"Thank you," Nikki said. "Wyatt, I know this may sound a bit forward, but where I come from in the future…well, people are a lot more direct about these things."

"I'm not sure what you're trying to say," he said.

"I…uh…this is a little embarrassing."

"Tell me. Please," said Earp, staring directly into her soft dark-brown eyes.

"I have this feeling about you, Wyatt," she said, "and not just because I knew you in the future, but…well, I just wanted you to know that I care about you a lot, and I want to help in any way I can."

"You're right," Earp said. "People don't talk about feelings and such in these parts, but I appreciate your honesty."

"Oh, I'm sorry," she said, moving closer to him and looking up into his big, twinkling eyes.

"I have a question," said Earp. "In this future you come from, were we ever…together?"

"Oh, no," she said. "I was way too young for that, and then I was dead."

"Yes. I could see how that might get in the way."

They both laughed.

"I'm alive now…and older," she said. "I'd say I'm around twenty-five, so it would be OK if you wanted to…" She paused.

Taking his cue, Sheriff Earp lowered his head, pulled Nikki close to him, and kissed her on the lips. She stood on her toes to reach him. Each found the kiss very pleasant, and they lingered for a few seconds before letting go and looking at each other, unable to move apart.

"Howdy, Sheriff!" yelled Niles, the butcher, from across the dusty street, breaking the spell.

"Greetings, Niles," said the sheriff, stepping back from Nikki. "How's the missus?"

"The same," he said. "Always complaining about the gout. Who's that you're talking with?"

"I'm Nikki," she said. "The sheriff's new deputy."

Niles kept walking, confused but quiet, until he disappeared into his shop.

"If it's OK," said Earp, "I'd like to ask for another kiss."

"It is," Nikki replied with a smile, and they kissed each other for a long time, sheltered under the wide brim of his hat.

"I think we need to keep our emotions in check, Nikki," he said when their lips finally parted. "If we're going to work together—I mean, like you suggested."

"Honestly," she said, in a bit of a daze, "I think I'll have a hard time keeping my hands off you."

"Best not to think about it too much," he said, and they kissed again as the sun set over the mountains in the west. "Let's see what happens."

"Evening, Sheriff," said the fashionably dressed Lillie Langtrees as she strolled by on her way to the saloon. She wore a pink silk dress with ruffles. "Am I interrupting anything?"

"Good evening, Lillie," Earp said. "You shouldn't be out wandering after dark."

"I could say the same about you," she said. "And your friend."

"May I introduce," said the sheriff, "Miss Nikki Hale."

"Miss Hale," Lillie said, extending her small hand. "I am Lillie Langtrees. I own that saloon and the whorehouse out yonder. If you're ever interested in a job, I could use another pretty girl like you."

"Nikki's not like that, Lillie," Earp said angrily. "She's a good girl."

"I'm very flattered by the offer, Miss Langtrees," said Nikki. "Obviously a woman of your age and experience would run a spectacular whorehouse, but Sheriff Earp has already offered me a job as his deputy."

"Oh, I see," said Lillie, eying Earp. "So, I take it you'll be hanging around my saloon looking for new ways to bust me, just like he does?"

"I'm afraid so," said Nikki.

"I'll take my leave, then," she said, turning to walk away. "Sheriff. Miss Hale."

"Evening, Lille," Earp said.

"Good night, Miss Langtrees," Nikki said. "And from now on, you can call me Red Ghost."

CHAPTER THIRTEEN

After a long day of riding and shooting with Rhino Bill Cody and Annie Oakley up in the mountains, Nikki Hale parted company with her new friends and rode her borrowed horse back to Sheriff Wyatt Earp's farm. She dismounted in front of the house, tied the horse to a post, and stood awhile longer, staring at the orange setting sun.

She'd spent the previous night with Earp, a man broken over the loss of his wife and hungry for something to replace the pain. Wyatt Earp—the one she had feelings for—was different from the other Wyatt Earp she'd worked with in the future. That Earp had been drunk most of the time and cranky, and he didn't seem to want or need anyone else in his life. None of that mattered to her now, though. She was happy.

When she reached the wooden porch, she saw that the screen door was half open.

"Wyatt, are you in there?"

No answer.

Nikki entered the small farmhouse and stopped in the living room to listen. Nothing. She looked into the kitchen and, finding no one there, walked to the bedroom and stopped. She thought she'd heard crying coming from inside the wardrobe.

"Wyatt?" she called out.

The wardrobe door was open a bit. She approached it slowly and put her hand on one of the doors, pulling it open, and…

A sudden crashing sound came from the living room. Nikki turned immediately and left the bedroom, confronting a very drunk Earp lying on the floor.

"Nikki…" He looked up and slurred, "I…fall down."

"Wyatt," she said, shocked. "Are you OK? I never expected to see you in this condition."

"It's my grieving," he said. "I only do it when I'm alone." Earp pulled himself up against the sofa.

"This is not right," said Nikki, firmly. "Now *and* in the future."

"Katie's gone," he said, tears glistening in his eyes. "I know I'll never see her again, but then you showed up…and it all came rushing back."

"I'm sorry, Wyatt, truly I am," said Nikki, sitting down next to him on the sofa. "If my being here is troubling you, I'll leave."

"No," he quickly said and took hold of her hand. "I want you to stay. Please."

Reaching up, he pulled her from the sofa, and they kissed, becoming more and more passionate. After a few minutes, they got up together and headed toward the bedroom at the end of the hall. As Earp sat on the soft, quilt-covered mahogany bed and drunkenly tried to pull off his boots, Nikki laughed and then pulled him down on top of her. They continued to kiss and began to undress. In the process, Earp noticed a bandage on Nikki's arm.

"What this?" he asked.

"Later," she replied, softly.

When they finished undressing, she pulled him against her naked skin. He pulled back the covers, and together they slid into the bed. He moved on top of her, kissing her mouth, neck, shoulders, and both her warm breasts, gently parting her legs and finally entering her. She began to moan. Putting her arms around Wyatt's neck, she looked up and smiled at him.

"Mmm...this feels so comfortable," she said, "except for maybe your six-gun that's poking me in the back. Do you think we can move it, Sheriff?"

"Kiss me," he said, sliding the gun off the bed.

They made love all night long.

* * *

"Wyatt," Nikki said softly, "I have to tell you something."

Earp's face was buried in a feather pillow, and he did not reply.

"Wyatt? Are you asleep?"

"Not any longer," he said.

It was around noon the next day, and Nikki was sitting up in bed, covered with a floral sheet of soft flannel.

Earp turned over to face her and smiled.

"Is this about work?" he asked, snuggling closer to Nikki. "Because I was having such a nice time in bed with my new deputy."

"No...seriously, Wyatt," she said. "When I was up in the hills with Bill and Annie yesterday, I ran into this smallish man who helped me after I was thrown by my horse."

"What happened?" asked Earp, sitting up in bed.

"I was attacked by big black birds, and they spooked my horse and I fell."

"You mean the bandage on your arm."

"Yes," she said.

"I'm listening."

"This little man who scared off the birds said his name was Bell," she said. "Then he asked if I wanted to see the old gold mine, the one where all the miners perished...where days ago he'd set off two underground bombs, and said he was back to check the site."

"Must have been the explosions we heard," said Earp. "Tell me more about this man, Bell."

"He said the bombs had been detonated a distance away from the mine using a device he invented."

"Why didn't you tell me about this last night?" he asked.

"You were too drunk to listen."

Earp got up and kissed Nikki, who got out of bed, wrapped her lower half in the sheet, and watched Wyatt walk naked to a chair by the window to pick up his folded trousers. A knock at the window diverted their attention.

"Good morning, lovebirds," said Annie, smiling and waving at both of them through the window. "Can we come in?"

Earp quickly pulled on his pants, and Nikki stepped behind the open wardrobe door to get dressed.

"Give us a few minutes, OK, Annie?" yelled Nikki as she reached for her trousers and shirt.

"Sure thing," said Rhino Bill, who was standing behind Annie. "Hope we didn't interrupt nothing."

"Go around to the front door," said Earp. "I'll let you in."

Earp made his way to the front of the house and opened the door. Annie walked in first, followed by Rhino Bill, who made himself comfortable leaning against the back wall.

"How you feel this morning, Sheriff?" asked Rhino Bill. "I mean, all the drinking you did last night at Miss Lillie's…"

"Don't remind me."

They sat down in the living room, a room that had been left pretty much untouched since Katie had disappeared years before.

"Nikki was telling me about a man she met yesterday in the hills," said Earp.

"Bell—Alex G. Bell, to be exact," said Nikki as she entered from the kitchen carrying a tea tray. "He said he was an inventor testing his bombs in the mountains."

"Inventor?" asked Annie, puzzled.

"Yes. He claimed to have created a device that allowed him to detonate the bombs from far away. He also told me he was afraid that the device he'd created was going to be used for some nefarious purpose and that he was powerless to stop it from happening."

"Ne-fa-ri-ous?"

"Did he say when this was going to happen?" asked Earp.

"Not directly, anyway," she said. "He only alluded to things—that he was working for a local man to pay off his debt, that he used to work for the railroad, and that he created a device to detonate bombs from a distance. When I pressed him further, he said he'd already told me too much and that I could be in danger if I found out any more. I believed him."

"Wonder why he told you that much," said Rhino Bill. "You being a stranger and all."

"I think he needed someone to talk to about his troubles," Nikki said. "And I just happened to cross his path."

"I've seen this Bell around town," said Earp, "and I'm pretty sure he works for Holliday. He could be the one behind all this bomb talk."

"Bell did say something I didn't quite understand," Nikki said. "If anyone found out he was talking to me, he would be killed and his body parts sold by the pound."

"Cadaver rustling," said Annie.

"Cadavers?" said Nikki. "Who wants to steal the dead?"

"Medical schools, hospitals, labs..." Earp said. "You'd be surprised. We've been investigating Holliday for various criminal activities, and selling cadavers is just one of them."

"Maybe this Bell guy is just plain crazy," said Rhino Bill.

"Crazy or not," said Sheriff Earp, "we're obliged to look into it. Holliday's been tied up in some pretty dirty business, including cheating people out of their land, kidnapping, and prostituting young girls at Miss Lillie's saloon. I just haven't been able to find any hard evidence or witnesses that tie him to a particular crime."

"I'm sure Bell would tell me more if I got closer to him," said Nikki. "He seemed so lost and alone that I'm sure I could get him to trust me."

"Could get messy," said Annie. "You'd better take my shotgun with you."

"Thanks, Annie," said Nikki, "I'll be just fine."

CHAPTER FOURTEEN

"Hello? It's Nikki Hale," she said as she walked into Alex G. Bell's lab located on the outskirts of town. "They said I could come in. I hope that's all right?"

"I'm glad to see you, Miss Hale," said Bell. "I'm surprised the guard let anyone in. I'm usually not allowed any visitors."

"I had no problem walking right by them," she said.

"Please sit down," said Bell, pulling out a chair for her.

"My goodness," Nikki said as she seated herself. "Your lab is *full* of interesting things. For instance, what is that over there on the shelf?"

"Oh, I'm very proud of that," said Bell.

It was a foot-tall, bronze-metal cylinder about two inches in diameter with a small bristle brush tied with twine to the top and a series of wires wrapped around its base.

"It's an electrical brush for cleaning teeth—you know, without moving the hand."

"That's crazy," said Nikki with a suppressed smile. "You invented the electric toothbrush?"

"And look what I have here," he said, indicating a large, rectangular metal box about a foot long that sat on the desk. "That is a device using magnetic waves to detonate bombs over long distances."

"Ah. That's why I'm here," she said. "When I met you in the hills, you were trying to tell me something about a crime that may or may not happen, and now you're showing me this device. Well, I think you may be in trouble."

"Trouble?"

"If someone is about to commit a heinous crime using your invention, Mr. Bell," she said.

"Call me, Alex," he said.

"You have to help me stop that from happening."

"I'm not sure what you mean," Bell said.

"Tell me who is behind this."

"He already knows all about you," said Bell, "and the sheriff, too—and that you've been snooping around town asking questions."

"*Who* knows?" she asked. "Tell me his name."

"He also knows that you're putting a team together to stop him," Bell said. "He called it a team full of prairie dogs and bastards."

"You seem to know a lot about him," she said. "But how do I know what you're telling me is true?"

"You'll just have to trust me," said Bell. "His spies are everywhere, and one of them overheard the drunken rhino hunter talking about forming a team last night when he was in the saloon."

"Who are his spies?" she asked. "Alex, you can't let innocent people die just because you're afraid of the consequences."

"I'm not brave, Nikki," he said. "Doc would kill me if I told you—"

"Doc?" she said. "Doc Holliday? Is *he* the one who's behind this—the man who's about to commit a heinous crime?"

"Yes."

"Tell me," she said. "Who is the target?"

"I don't know," said Bell. "He doesn't trust me."

"Listen, I just had an idea," said Nikki. "Why don't you join us?"

"Join you?"

"The Protectors," she said. "Be on the team."

"I don't have any special skills," he said. "What would I do?"

"You're an inventor, right? I'll bet you could create many useful gadgets that would be an asset to the team."

"As a matter of fact," he said, "I *am* working on a mechanical instrument that could connect the world."

"I'd have to check with the rest of the team first," she said. "But from what I've seen and heard, you'd be a valuable member of the team."

"I'm afraid, though," he said sadly, "my days as a living, breathing inventor are numbered. I've been living on borrowed time ever since I became indebted to Doc Holliday. The only way out is to pay the man off."

"There's another way," she said. "We can keep you safe in the Protectors. You'll just disappear and become one of us."

"As tempting as that sounds," said Bell, "Holliday is a savage killer, and I'm more afraid of him than of you."

"OK," she said. "You mentioned you didn't know *who* Holliday's target was, but do you know when it will happen?"

"Very soon," he said. "The detonation device is finished, and he's been after me to give him the bomb. But so far I've been able to put him off."

"See?" she said. "You're already trying to help."

"I'm not one of the bad guys, Nikki," he said. "You're looking at somebody who just got in way over his head."

"Could you defuse it?" she asked.

"What?"

"The bomb? If you can detonate it over long distances, what about the reverse? Defuse it so it doesn't blow up?"

"I'd have to think about it," Bell said. "Holliday is a powerful man, and he doesn't like to be tricked. He said if I crossed him, he'd shoot me!"

"He's just a man, Alex," said Nikki. "And he can be stopped."

"I'm not so sure," said Bell. "He's a madman who's close to getting a bomb that can be exploded far away from the scene of the crime. He might be a little more difficult to bring down than you think."

"Thank you, ladies and gentlemen," said Madam G from the stage.

Applause.

It was the final night before Leader Garfield's train trip west.

"Thank you very much," he said. "And welcome to our last show at the Capital Club for the season."

Applause, and more applause.

Madam G stood in a bright-blue floral gown, his wig of long auburn curls pulled back behind his head, wearing face powder and rouge in quantities perfect for the spotlight. The gown was floor length, exposing only the bottoms of the high-heeled black shoes he wore, and a fox-fur stole covered his naked shoulders.

"I know you're as disappointed as I am that this is the last show" he said, "but it's going to be a great one."

"What do you think, Jonny?" Madam G asked his accompanist. "Ladies and gentlemen, let's give a round of applause for my better half, Jonny—my man at the keyboard."

Applause.

"Thank you. My opening number is an old favorite by that great southern composer, Stephen Foster, and it's called...Jonny, if you please."

Jonny began to play, and Madam G sang:

I dream of Jeanie with the light-brown hair,
Borne, like a vapor, on the summer air;
I see her tripping where the bright streams play,
Happy as the daisies that dance on her way.
Many were the wild notes her merry voice would pour.
Many were the blithe birds that warbled them o'er:
Oh! I dream of Jeanie with the light-brown hair,
Floating, like a vapor, on the soft summer air.

"You have such passionate eyes, Lillie," said Doc Holliday from under the sheets.

"Too bad they're wasted looking at you," Lillie Langtrees said, turning to face the sunlit view of the western mountains beyond. "You're ugly both inside and out."

Holliday sat up, picked up and pulled on his trousers, and then stood up from the bed.

"You only say coldhearted things like that to hurt me, Lillie," he said, "because you know I love you."

"Coldhearted? I take that as a compliment."

She stood up naked before the two curtainless windows, exposing her milky white-pink flesh and the long, soft, twisted curls on her head.

"Yes," he said. "You would. I've never met another person who is as ruthless as I am, but you sure come close."

Stepping closer to the window, Lillie gazed upon a team of workers stationed behind the saloon. They were slaughtering pigs, cutting them up into pieces and throwing the waste into a shallow pit. Noticing Lillie standing naked in the window, some of the workers stared up at her, and she moved her body as if in a dance, shaking her hips and fully exposing her privates.

"I hope they're enjoying the show," said Holliday as he returned to the dresser, picked up a rolled cigarette, and lit it from a burning candle. "'Cause I'm the one who's paying for it."

She turned slowly, giving the workers below a tantalizing glimpse of her derrière.

"A free show always brings in more business," she said. "And after they're paid, they'll have money to spend on drink and girls."

"Always thinking about business, eh, Lillie?"

"Someone has to," she said, continuing to shake her derrière. "You waste so much on your revenge schemes. Why don't you focus more on making instead of spending money?"

"And you, my lovely," he said, "have a rather large rear."

"I don't see *them* complaining."

Lillie stopped dancing, picked up her robe from the bed, and put it on.

"I don't care about the business," said Holliday.

"That's because you were born into wealth."

"It's my family's honor that's at stake," he said. He put on his shirt and shoes and stubbed out his cigarette. "And nothing will deter me from my mission to kill the one responsible."

"I don't need to know any more," she said. "But since we're business partners, you'd better tell me your plan so that I can make one of my own, just in case."

"Just in case?"

"In case your plan fails."

Lillie walked over to a delicately carved desk and sat down on a high-backed chair covered in silk brocade. Holliday followed suit, sitting in the chair opposite. She opened a cigar box on her desk, took out a long brown cigar, clipped off the end, and used a lit candle to light it. She took a long drag and blew smoke out in circles that drifted above their heads.

"OK," she said. "I'm listening."

"In a few days," he said, "I'll be taking my Resurrectionists to Prairie Junction to meet up with Damian, the lead man who went on ahead a few days ago to scout the place and secure lodgings for us. Once we get set up, it will be a matter of only a day or two before the coward arrives."

"And who is this coward?"

"Garfield," Holliday spit out.

"Keep going," she said impatiently.

"He will be traveling on private train with his family," Holliday said, "and stopping at Prairie Junction to take on water before heading off on the weeks-long journey to the western coast. That's where we'll hit him—just outside of town."

"I can't believe you could be so stupid!" she said. "Have you thought about all the security that will be surrounding the Leader on his travels? How do you plan to get around that?"

"As always, my love," Holliday said with a broad smile, "I am two steps ahead of you. My man will be planted on the train, just waiting for me to give the order to strike. Now, with my bomb almost complete, my revenge is at hand."

"And what about me?" she asked. "Where do *I* fit into your plan?"

"We'll be gone."

"Gone? Gone where?"

"Anywhere you'd like," he said, standing up. "Atlantica Continent?"

"And you think the sheriff is going to let you get away with this?"

"The sheriff is chasing his tail," Holliday said. "I'm not worried about him...or his new gang."

"And why not?"

"Because I've buried five heavy-duty bombs of my own under Ghost Town, and I intend to use Bell's long-distance device to explode them all after I return from destroying Garfield. You'd better get packing, because anything you leave behind will be lost in the blast."

"How much time do I have?" Lillie asked.

"Not much," he said. "The train is coming through Prairie Junction in a matter of days, and then it will all be over—the horrible headaches I suffer, the snide looks I get from the people in town even though I'm the mayor and should be respected. And the man responsible for the death of my parents and family, Leader James A. Garfield, along with his family, will be blown into dust."

CHAPTER FIFTEEN

The gothic-looking train station in Washington, DC, was enveloped in a swirling sea of steam that poured out of idling trains. It shrouded the crowds—the peddlers, the people working, the many others traveling, and still others there to send off Leader James A. Garfield, the young man who had gone from foot soldier in the Great War to Leader of the great continent of Nena within a thirteen-year time span. They worshiped him for his success. Garfield, traveling with his wife, Lucretia; their twin boys, Harry Augustus and James Jr.; and the newest addition, baby Louise in her pram, was surrounded by government soldiers, almost twenty-five of them, all wearing blue uniforms with black belts, boots, and caps. The Leader's train sat in the middle track, its tail end covered in local and national flags. In front of it, a wooden platform had been built, and from this perch, Leader Garfield stood and waved to the large crowd gathered to say good-bye. Lucretia stood next to him holding Louise, and the twin boys stood on either side of their father.

"Leader Garfield?" a member of the press contingent asked. "Is it true that the purpose of your trip is to seek the counsel of a clairvoyant who can get rid of your family ghost?"

"I'm not sure what you are talking about, my good fellow," said Garfield. "My intentions out west are to visit as many of the locals as I can and perhaps meet members of the various indigenous tribes. After all, I am Leader of the *entire* continent."

"Leader?" one reporter called out. "Some say you're trapped by your ideology, and it's been reported that many of your fellow politicians are not happy with your new inclusive policies to force change. Some are even vowing to take revenge. Is there any truth to that rumor?"

"Many of my fellow politicians are unhappy with change," said Garfield. "And they feel it will compromise their power. I for one think that is a good thing."

"Sir!" another press reporter yelled. "Is it true that there's another woman in your life? A certain tall, torch singer named Madam G who works at the Capital Club?"

Garfield glanced at his wife and then looked out at the crowd.

"No comment."

"All aboard!" signaled the train's conductor. A loud steam whistle blew shrilly, accompanied by waves of billowing steam.

"Well, ladies and gentlemen," shouted Leader Garfield above the din, "until we meet again, I bid you all farewell."

Garfield and his family left the platform, climbed the stairs to the train, waved to the dispersing crowd, and then moved inside, followed by a smaller contingent of guards and the staff that would accompany them on their long journey out west. With a *toot-toot!* of the whistle, the train lunged forward out of the station, heading first south and then turning west, the direction it would follow until it ended up on the sparsely populated western shore of the Nena Continent.

Inside, the Leader and his wife lived comfortably in the sleeping car; their children bunked in the next car. Both cars were behind the office car, the dining car, the staff car, and the steam engine up front that pulled the entire train along the tracks.

"I'm glad we didn't invite the press along," said Garfield to his wife.

"They're so nosy and ask way too many personal questions."

"Imagine if they ever found out the mysterious Madam G is actually their Leader!" said Lucretia, laughing. "There'd be a riot."

"I've given up pretty much everything else to be the Leader," said Garfield. "I have so few things left that are close to my heart, and one of them is singing."

"I don't understand it," said Lucretia, "but I support you as my husband."

"Sir," said General Georgia, the senior officer on the train upon entering the car. "Our spies have intercepted a secret communiqué that mentions an assassination attempt on a very senior official, so we'd better not take any chances. You need to cancel this trip and turn around before we go too far out."

"Nonsense, General," said Garfield. "I'm not moved by vague threats. We will not turn back."

"Maybe you should listen to the general, James," said Lucretia. "She sounds very sure there is reason to be concerned."

"My dear," Garfield said, "there have been numerous death threats against me, and I have not given in to a single one—and I never will."

"Sir, please," General Georgia said. "My top priority is to protect you and your family on this train from harm, real or imagined, so I must insist that you—"

"At ease, General," Garfield said. "I'm the captain of this ship. I'll say where and when we go."

"Yes, sir. May I be dismissed?" asked General Georgia. "I need to telewire security about our upcoming arrival in New Canton to refuel."

"You may," Garfield said, "but stay close in case there is any truth to this assassination attempt."

The general turned stiffly and marched to the door, where she turned back, bowed at the waist, walked out, and closed the door behind her.

"That woman gives me the creeps," said Lucretia.

"She's just doing her job, dear," Garfield said. "Annoying as it may be."

"Maybe she has a point, though, James. If someone is trying to assassinate you, perhaps we should consult with a paranormal adviser."

"You mean like Dr. Warlock?" asked Garfield. "That didn't work out too well the first time, did it?"

"He got rid of mother's ghost," said Lucretia.

"Yes," said Garfield. "But he pretty much destroyed our home in the process."

"Do you believe Alex Bell can be trusted, Nikki?" asked Sheriff Wyatt Earp, holding her in his strong arms as they stood at the back of the jail and watched the sunset.

"Yes, I do," Nikki Hale said and then kissed him softly on his lips. "He seems remorseful about his role in all this—and too terrified of Doc Holliday to stop. Frankly, Bell seems pretty much terrified of everything."

"We might be able to use his fear to our advantage," said Earp. "You told him that we'd protect him if he wanted to join our side?"

"I did," she said, "but he said we're too few, that Holliday and his gang of Resurrectionists number in the teens. He may be right."

"This is not the time to panic," said Earp. "We need to develop our own plan."

"I agree. But if Holliday is the one who's planning to use this long-distance detonation device and bomb to kill someone—or many people—we need to find out who his target is."

"Bell's sure it's Holliday behind all this?"

"Yes," Nikki said. "He told me that when Holliday was younger, he was the one responsible for the explosion that caused the gold mine to cave in, trapping those miners. Does that sound plausible?"

"Only if we can prove it."

"Bell was sure Holliday would kill him before he'd let him join our side."

"Then we need to convince Bell to become a double agent," said Earp. "He's already close to Holliday and may be able to relay anything he finds out about the intended target back to us through you."

"Smart."

"Do you think you can get him to do that, Nikki?" asked Earp.

She paused. "Before I answer, may I have another kiss?"

He complied, and they kissed passionately.

"I can continue trying to convince him to be part of our group," she said, "but he'll only join if we can guarantee his safety, and I'm not sure we can."

"We can do it," Earp said, forcefully.

"Wyatt, are you sure? Even with Bell, that only makes five of us against Holliday's gang. I think we need some outside help. We need to call in the government."

"I've sent for Iron Weed."

"Who?"

"Chief Iron Weed," said Earp. "He's an old friend and said he'd be here tomorrow with at least five of his followers. That will give us much better odds."

"And who is Chief Iron Weed?"

"An elemental shaman," Earp said. "He can read animal bones."

"I still think we need an army."

"I'm not sure we can trust anyone on this, Nikki. If Holliday has as much power as Bell says, who's to say he hasn't already planted his spies in the government?"

"I see your point, Wyatt," she said. "But we do need more help."

"We're Protectors now, Nikki," said Earp. "We're on our own."

"I guess we are," she said. "And, I'm glad we're doing this together."

They kissed with passion, and then it was dark.

The new Protectors—gunslinger Sheriff Wyatt Earp; the espionage expert Nikki Hale; animal spirit guide Rhino Bill Cody; and his wife, the teen sharpshooter Annie Oakley—were seated in Earp's living room. The latest arrival to the first Protectors team meeting, Chief Iron Weed, sat on the floor, while his five heavily armed bodyguards stood outside and watched for any sign of trouble. The chief shook a small leather bag of animal bones he carried and cast them on the floor.

"Chief?"

"Nothing," he said. "The bones do not seem to be talking to me today, but I will keep trying."

"Since this is our first official Protectors meeting," said Earp, "I'd like to welcome you all here. I'm real excited about our first assignment—stopping a madman from blowing up an innocent person or persons with a bomb he can detonate from a distance."

"By madman," said Nikki, "he means Doc Holliday."

"Thanks," said Annie.

"Who do you think it is he's tryin' to kill, Sheriff?" asked Rhino Bill.

"Leader James A. Garfield," Earp said. "Ruler of Nena Continent."

"What makes you figure that?" asked Rhino Bill. "That's a pretty steep climb."

"Inventor Alex G. Bell," Nikki said. "He told me about an incident from Holliday's youth that led Wyatt and me to do a little research in the old Ghost Town archives stored in the jail."

"We found old news clippings," said Earp, "some going way back to the town's formation, and discovered that Holliday's family borrowed a large sum of money from back east and were evicted from their longtime home for nonpayment of the loan by a young banker named—"

"Holliday!" Annie shouted out.

"No—Garfield," said the sheriff. "If my theory is correct and Holliday is the one seeking revenge against the Leader, then a lot of innocent people around him will get killed when his bomb explodes."

"That's horrible!" said Annie.

"Shouldn't we get help?" asked Rhino Bill.

"That's what I said," Nikki said, "but Wyatt convinced me otherwise."

"I'll bet he did, darlin'," said Annie with a wink. "I'll bet he did."

"I wish we had proof," said Rhino Bill. "Not that I don't believe you two, but the Leader lives very far away from here and all."

"He's on a road trip," said Earp. "I reached out to someone I trust by telewire and found out Leader Garfield is traveling by steam train, and one of the watering stations where he has to stop and refuel is just sixty miles away from here, and I think that's where the Protectors need to be."

"Perfect place for an ambush," said Rhino Bill. "The object of Holliday's revenge will be close at hand."

"See," said Nikki, "that's why Wyatt and I believe it. Holliday has the motive, and now he has the opportunity."

"The evidence keeps piling up," said Annie. "I'm a-gettin' hungry."

"Iron Weed," said Earp, "are you and your men in with us?"

The chief shook his bag of bones and spilled them on the floor.

"The bones tell me to join you," said the chief. "And this man...Bell? He holds the key to our success."

CHAPTER SIXTEEN

Lillie Langtrees stood in front of her saloon under an extended awning that shielded her fair pink-white skin from the harsh noonday sun as she peered up and down the deserted Ghost Town street. As she moved, the dry prairie midday breeze tousled her light-brown curls, the ones on her forehead fluttering like silent bells.

From down the street came four horsemen, all dressed in black, including scarves that cover the lower half of their faces. They stopped in front of Lillie.

"What do you want here?" she called out.

"Waiting for the boss," one of the horsemen said.

"Usually you Resurrectionists stay away from town," said Lillie. "Except maybe when you need to pick up a body."

The door behind Lillie swung open with a bang, and Doc Holliday emerged, followed by the town's blacksmith.

"Otis, I need these four horses and my own ready by morning," said Holliday.

"You can pick 'em up at dawn," Otis said. "I'll work all night."

The four Resurrectionists dismounted and walked into the saloon.

"Don't touch anything without paying for it," said Lillie as they passed.

Otis took the horses' reins and walked off down the street toward the stable, soon disappearing inside.

"How can you associate with men that sell the dead?" Lillie asked as Holliday moved closer.

"Forget about them," he said. "They're just security. Now, how about a kiss?"

"Here, in public?" she said. "With you?"

"I'm as good as any," he said, grabbing her. "Good enough to drink at your saloon."

"Yes, I can smell that you've had quite a few," said Lillie. "I hope you paid."

"You're cruel." Holliday tried to kiss her but missed as she turned her pink-rouged cheek away. "It's a long journey to Prairie Junction, and I need a kiss before I go."

"Better that you kiss a goat than me," she said. "There's one out back."

"I'm hurt," he said.

"Now," she said, pushing him away, "enough of this nonsense. Tell me, when can I expect Sheriff Earp to be out of my way? You're leaving tomorrow, but I'll be stuck here with him poking around and annoying the customers while you're away."

"Kiss first," he said. "I'll pay later."

"Not today," she said. "I have a headache."

"You and your headaches," he snapped. "You should look into that. Might be a case of brain fever."

"I doubt that," she said. "When will you be back?"

"Uh…there's been a slight change in my plans," said Holliday, nervously. "I won't be coming back to Ghost Town."

"You said you'd get rid of Earp at the same time you disposed of Garfield!" Lillie shouted. "And what about the bombs you buried under the town?"

"I no longer care about Sheriff Earp or Ghost Town," said Holliday, cavalierly. "But if you wanted to kill him yourself, don't let me stand in your way."

—•—

"I'm frozen with fear, Nikki," Alex G. Bell said. "I'd like to believe what you're saying, but I've seen firsthand what horrors Doc Holliday has inflicted on others. He's a cruel sadist who cares nothing for human life—except maybe as playthings. By the way, how did you get in here? This lab is heavily guarded. Even I can't get out."

"I'm not Nikki anymore, Alex," she said. "I'm Red Ghost. I have the ability to be seen only when I want to be. I walked right past your guards without being noticed."

"That's pretty amazing, considering you're wearing a red satin sash tied around her waist," he said. "What do you want of me, Nikki…uh, Red Ghost?"

"Alex," she said, "you sit at a desk in a building that Doc Holliday paid for, crying to me that you're afraid to do the right thing. Well, guess what, Alex? We're all afraid, so get over it."

"Easy for you to say," he said. "You can disappear, and I'll be stuck here, a sitting target. I just want to flee."

"Alex, being frightened all the time must be exhausting," she said, positioning her face not three inches from Bell's. "Now is the time to stop worrying about things that may never happen and use all that wasted energy to make things right. Understood?"

"Yes," he said, quietly. "I'm too embarrassed to admit it, but you're right. I am my own worst enemy, blaming Holliday for my fate when I was just afraid of taking responsibility."

"We're all alike inside, Alex," said Nikki. "We're all human and have many virtues and many flaws, and we all make mistakes. The point is to learn from them to fix things. It's never too late."

"I..."

Bell couldn't continue his thought. Instead, he got up from his chair and walked over to the window. Outside, the long prairie desert vista unfolded before him—miles upon miles of brown-gray-green-colored scrub grass, cactus, and tumbleweed.

"Come over here," he said, stepping away from the window toward a tabletop in another part of his lab. "I want to show you something,"

Nikki followed, and Bell handed her something—a rectangular object made of bronze about the size of a clenched fist, only flatter.

"What is this?" she asked, turning the object around in her hand.

"The last time we met," he said, "you said some very thought-provoking things and...well, I've been working in secret on a rudimentary handheld communication device that is small enough for each of you to carry without its being burdensome."

"That's amazing, Alex! How does it work?"

"The devices will be wirelessly connected to the electromagnetic current that travels underground. It will tap into this current, turning it into a code of sorts that is shared among all the devices and translated into language for the recipients. With a little training, the Protectors should be able to develop their own common language to communicate with one another over great distances that no one else can intercept."

"This settles it, Alex," Nikki said. "We need your expertise and bravery on the team."

"Bravery?" he said, flustered. "I mean...I accept."

"Congratulations! You're our newest member."

"What happens now?" Bell asked. "Do we escape? Can you get me out of here with your vanishing powers?"

"My what? No, my skill comes from a lifetime of physical training, not from magic."

"I'm ready," Bell said, confidently. "What do we do next?"

"The Protectors have a plan." She leaned over and whispered into Bell's ear. "Here's what we want you to do..."

New Canton, a gateway city to the southwest, was the first major destination on Leader Garfield's trip, and it turned out to be a very bad place—the scene of not one but two assassination attempts on the Leader's life, both at the same event.

A little more than a day into the Leader's train trip, the eastern press grew weary of being excluded from the popular story and turned its attention to the opposition party and its outspoken leader, Mable Stone. Stone, a sturdily built woman standing five feet four with short-cropped brown hair, green eyes, and a husky voice, was the daughter of wealthy Judge Stone, who through graft and extortion had made himself rich, influencing cases and deciding outcomes based on his whim and what he was paid under the table. At one time, it was thought no one could stop his corrupt ways—or those of his equally pugnacious daughter, Mable.

The Leader's steam train pulled into New Canton, in the late afternoon, after the brightest sun had already set. With the *toot* of a whistle, the train's steam covered the awaiting crowd of more than fifty people with a gloomy gray mist that seemed to mirror the mood. After it dissipated, there stood Leader Garfield and his wife, Lucretia, holding their baby, Louise, flanked by their sons, Harry Augustus and James Jr., wearing gold-buttoned blue uniforms to match their father's. When all three saluted the crowd, it roared its approval. Then Leader Garfield took off his hat and waved it to the crowd.

Cheers.

In front of the train, water poured into the steam engine through a giant spout from a nearby tower as the train rested before beginning the next leg of its journey south toward Prairie Junction to rewater before setting out across the long, dry desert that lay westward.

People in the front row hushed the rest, and the Leader stepped forward.

"My fellow New Cantonians," Garfield shouted to the crowd. "I am so pleased to be here with you today during this celebration in my honor, and I would like to thank you all from myself and my family for taking the time to come out to see us as we make our way through this great continent of ours and make history—the first Leader ever to travel coast to coast!"

More cheers from the crowd.

"Leader Garfield!" a press reporter called out. "Mrs. Stone has accused you of using your office for personal gain, saying that your wealth comes from accounts set up in your wife's name. Is there any truth to her statement?"

"Mable Stone," said the Leader, "has decided to engage me by spreading false stories and leaks to the press to further her own campaign against me for the position of Leader. I can unequivocally say that her accusations are baseless."

"I'd like to thank the Leader for taking time out of his busy schedule to be with us here today," said New Canton's mayor, Chika Bushby, who stood on the train platform alongside Garfield. "Now I'd like to invite you to follow me—"

"Garfield killed my father!" a young male voice shouted from somewhere in the crowd, which was now beginning to panic.

Then a gunshot rang out, and hit the mayor in the chest, close to her heart. She fell forward and over the rail of the parked train.

Someone screamed.

The Leader's guard surrounded him and his family, huddling them back into the train. The crowd ran in the opposite direction, away from the station, causing mayhem in the streets.

Then another shot rang out and hit General Georgia, killing her instantly.

"Garfield is a murderer!" shouted a teenage boy standing in position and pointing a handgun at the train.

"Tell Garfield," said the teen, "Mable Stone says hello."

He then turned the gun around on himself and pulled the trigger, blowing the top of his head off. Inside the train, seated at a long table covered with food, Garfield and his family were shaken but not deterred from their meet-and-greet tour of the citizens of Nena Continent.

"Did you see that young anarchist with the gun?" asked Lucretia, passing the mashed turnips. "Shameful. A lunatic out in public."

"Yes," said Garfield, licking his fingers, reluctant to incite her.

"Lunatic," repeated young Harry Augustus, chewing on a roll.

"See?" Garfield said. "You need to be careful what you say in front of the children."

"That boy was aiming at you," she said. "Luckily, he missed."

"Not so lucky for the mayor and General Georgia, I'm afraid," said the Leader.

"I can't worry about everyone," said Lucretia. "And now I have a chill."

Lucretia got up to get a shawl from the back of the long railroad car while the family continued to eat without her. A few minutes later, though...

"Where is Lucretia?" asked Garfield. "Where is your mother?"

"Over here," said a female voice near the door. Garfield turned to see a woman in a green bonnet and matching dress holding a long, sharp knife to Lucretia's throat and dragging her out by her hair onto the platform between trains. "We are the Anarchists!"

Bam! A shot whizzed and hit the woman's forehead dead center, so clean it barely bloodied her bonnet. She fell off the platform, and Lucretia ran to Leader Garfield.

"The children?" she asked.

"Safe," he said.

The conductor, a tall, lean man with a shaved head, had shot the woman holding the knife to Lucretia's throat. She, along with the teen with the gun, had been sent by Mable Stone to kill Garfield's entire family, thereby eliminating her competition.

"Tell the engineer we're ready to leave," said Garfield. "And, thanks."

"All aboard!" yelled the conductor after he stepped out of the train.

The security personnel boarded the train, blocking some of the press that had lingered. After everyone was on board, the conductor bent over to pick up the footstool from under the trains' bottom step, and he felt something sharp pierce his back. A tall bald man dressed all in black held a sharp, shiny knife, which had cut through the conductor's clothes, flesh, muscle, bone, and even several major internal organs, killing him almost instantly. His body fell to the ground.

The man who'd stabbed him was Damian, Doc Holliday's henchman and the leader of the Resurrectionists. Damian put the knife away and then dragged the conductor's body under the train on the next track. On the way back, Damian picked up the conductor's cap and placed it on his own head.

"All aboard!" shouted Damian, the new conductor, as he stepped back on the train. It pulled slowly out of the New Canton station, heading south to Prairie Junction before the big push out west.

CHAPTER SEVENTEEN

The late-night silence was pierced by the screams of a woman that could be heard up and down the deserted main street in Ghost Town. The screams were coming from the upstairs apartment of Lillie Langtrees's saloon. It was Lillie herself who was screaming as she gave birth to her sisters, the almost duplicates she'd formed from her genetic makeup. That was her special talent.

She sat in a bloody pool of discharge, the result of her lower abdomen being ripped wide open and her organs moving around on the inside.

Squeal!

Then came a louder squeal, and another, and another, as four naked, bloody humanoid balls of flesh squirmed on the floor. The piglets didn't really look like babies at all but rather like small loaves of bread. They lapped up the blood and within seconds grew noticeably larger in size.

"Arise, my sisters," Lillie said as her insides began healing by themselves. "Windi, Terra, Ginger, and Oceanna—we have work to do."

The largest one grew quickly into a shapely woman who looked similar to Lillie but had different coloring and personality. Windi had long, straight blond hair and blue eyes as well as the power to create storms and gale-force winds and could glide in small breezes. Her sister Terra could cause earthquakes, avalanches, and earth tremors by pressing the ground and channeling the volcanoes erupting underneath. She had short black hair and dark-brown eyes and was very shy. A third sister, an aggressive redheaded fire-starter named Ginger, could emit flames from her pores and throw fireballs she could create in the palms of her hands. And the last, a sister who went by the name of Oceanna, could control moisture, water, and rain. She had shoulder-length white hair and reddish-pink eyes.

"Hurry," Lillie begged her sisters. "The sheriff is coming."

In a matter of moments, the Langtrees sisters were fully grown, reaching five feet, two and a quarter inches in height—almost a tall as their host, Lillie.

"I hate that part," said Ginger, who stood up, naked. "Crawling around like grubs on the floor."

"What do we have to wear?" asked Oceanna, sitting up and wrapping her arms around her knees.

"I'm hungry," said Terra. She also stood up and looked around.

"What's up?" asked Windi.

"We need to kill the sheriff," Lillie said. "Then get out of town."

"That Sheriff Earp is sure good-looking," said Windi, blowing on the floor to dry up any remaining blood. "I'd like to meet him...you know, alone."

"Down, girl," said Ginger. "A sister's got to share."

"Be careful what you say, Ginger," said Windi, "or I'll huff, and I'll puff, and I'll blow you right out."

"Let's keep this moving," said Lillie. "There'll be time for infighting after we're done. Stop arguing and get dressed."

One by one, Windi, Oceanna, Terra, and Ginger walked naked into a large closet in the back of Lillie's bedroom and emerged dressed in different-colored silk outfits covered with lace and feathers—the same as the original worn by Lillie herself.

"The Langtrees sisters," said Ginger as they prepared to do battle with the law, "are ready to rumble."

"Mr. Holliday," said the old man at the desk. "What are you doing here?"

En route to Prairie Junction to meet the Leader's train, Doc Holliday surprised his workers at the human body bank run by the Resurrectionists located on the outskirts of Ghost Town. It was hidden away in a giant salt cave that had been discovered by gold miners years before. Now it was used to keep the bodies fresh for the long journey back east to medical schools and hospitals, where they would be used for training.

"I'm here to check up on you boys," said Holliday. "Looks kinda slow."

"Well," said the old man at the desk, "We've been having some problems finding fresh bodies, so you know business has dropped off."

"Has it?" said Holliday, as cool as a cucumber. "Where's Damian?"

"He's not here," the man said. "You sent him ahead to get on the train."

"That's right," said Holliday, reaching over the counter to grab the old man by the collar and lifting him up out of his chair. "And while he's away, I expect my business to continue as is, or else the whole lot of you will be...replaced."

"Yeah," said the old man, trying to pull away. "I get what you're saying, boss, but we can't find any bodies to sell."

"Then *make* some," said Holliday. "Use some ingenuity, a little brainpower, to come up with a plan to get more."

"Uh..." he mumbled, "I'm not sure what you're saying."

"If you need more bodies, the obvious way to get them is to kill them yourself. Create a body pool of your own. Start with society's rejects—

the poor, the old, and the defenseless young. Babies bring in higher prices, by the way, so form a plan and then take action to get as many bodies as you are able to sell."

"Got ya, boss," he said. "Just kill 'em."

Inside the entrance to the salt cave, Holliday and his two bodyguards, Ben and Terry, passed a line of covered horse-drawn wagons that were being loaded with what looked like wrapped mummies.

"How long before you leave?" Holliday asked a young man loading a wagon.

"About an hour."

"If you can cut that time in half," said Holliday, "I'll double your pay."

"Seriously?" the man asked. "And what about the rest of my men?"

"Same deal," he called out for all to hear. "Double the speed, and I'll double your pay."

Holliday and his bodyguards walked farther into the cave, following a lit string of kerosene-filled lanterns that ran the length of the shaft walls on both sides and illuminated the cave in soft, dreamy light. Train tracks ran down the center of the floor and disappeared into the dark depths. The tracks were used to carry small, bullet-shaped railroad cars that could transport up to thirty dead bodies, maintenance equipment, and bags of salt up and down the length of the cave.

"Something stinks in there!" said Ben, turning away.

"Yeah," said Terry as he held his nose. "Smells like rotting meat."

"Gentlemen," said Holliday, "or should I call you ladies?"

"And look at all the dead people," said Ben. "It's unsettling, boss."

Holliday pulled his pearl-handled six-gun from its holster and pointed it in Ben's face. "More unsettling than my shooting you through the head at close range?"

"No, boss," said Ben, looking down at his feet.

Holliday lowered his gun and walked a short distance ahead. His two bodyguards followed.

"On your right, gentlemen," said Holliday, pointing, "is the reason for the pungent odor—the unsalted dead."

Ten feet away from them sat two carloads of decaying bodies, some clothed, others naked, and all in a state of decay.

Terry vomited.

"The smell!" said Ben. "Boss, please—let's go."

"After they've had their salt bath," said Holliday, "when all the moisture is removed from their decaying flesh, the smell of rotting death will disappear, and they will be placed in the salt vaults to cure until they are shipped. Now, let's get out of here. My revenge is at hand!"

* * *

"Hear me, sisters," called Lillie Langtrees, one leg up on her satin-covered stool, to her four almost duplicates. "That sniveling coward Doc Holliday has abandoned us—left us here alone to fend for ourselves. Well, sisters, we cannot be intimidated, and we—"

"That rodent turd!" said Ginger. "Who does he think he is?"

"I knew he couldn't be trusted," said Oceanna. "Beady eyes and small, narrow lips."

"Let's kill him, sisters," said Terra. "Crush him like a kitten."

"Why waste your time, sister?" asked Windi. "There are other fish in the sea."

"Are you making fun of me?" asked Oceanna. "'Cause I'm made of water?"

"Relax," said Ginger. "Let Lillie speak."

"I've moved on," said Lillie. "We don't need Holliday anymore, and frankly, we never did. Our real threat is that pesky sheriff and his gang of amateurs. They must be stopped, or we will all end up incarcerated in a dirty, smelly prison—or worse."

"What's worse than being locked away with you lot?" asked Oceanna, dressed in a deep-blue dress with a matching bonnet.

"Being dead," said Windi, the blonde in a yellow silk day dress who sat demurely on the left side of the bed.

"It won't be easy to defeat Earp," said Terra. "Especially now that he has help."

"What's the plan, sister?" asked Ginger, who wore a royal-red dress. She snapped her fingers, igniting them into small flames. "I'm ready for some action."

"The plan is to surprise, overwhelm, and then bury them in the desert where no one will ever find them," said Lillie, who was dressed all in white. "Then we leave with all the gold I've saved and start a new life on the coast."

"I'd like to kill somebody today," said Windi. "I don't much care who it is."

"Why do you always need to kill, Windi?" asked Terra.

"Because I enjoy it," she said. "Same as you."

"Give it a rest, will ya?" said Ginger, walking over to the window. "Lillie said we ain't got time to fight among ourselves."

"Ginger?" asked Oceanna. "The voice of reason?"

"Hey!" Ginger yelled, looking out the window. "You can forget about surprising them—Earp and gang are right outside."

The sisters scrambled all over the bedroom to find their weapons and then rushed to the windows.

Outside, Sheriff Earp, Nikki Hale, Rhino Bill Cody, and Annie Oakley cautiously approached Lillie's saloon on horseback.

"We might be walking into a trap here, Sheriff," said Rhino Bill.

"If it's not," Nikki said, "I'm sure they've seen us by now."

"The plan is to take out Lillie and her sisters first," said Earp. "Then we go after Doc Holliday."

"Thanks for reminding me," said Annie. "By the way, a gun's pointing at us from up in that window yonder."

Windi used her rifle butt and smashed the glass and then fired off multiple shots at the approaching Protectors in the street below.

"Look out!" yelled Rhino Bill. "They're shootin' at us!"

Next, Terra broke the glass in the next window and fired a pistol at Nikki, who somersaulted off her horse and out of the way. On her feet quickly, she ran to a drainpipe and climbed up to the saloon's front roof.

"She's mine!" shouted Terra, jumping out the window and onto the roof, intent on confronting Nikki.

Down below, the Protectors scattered—Earp under the saloon's front porch, Rhino Bill behind an abandoned wagon left in the middle of Main Street, and Annie alongside her palomino horse.

On the roof, Terra threw the first punch, which Nikki dodged, and then missed with a second.

"Get out of the way, sister," said Windi, "so I can get a clean shot."

Nikki hit back, knocking Terra down. Windi cocked her rifle, aimed through the window, and fired, missing Nikki, who moved a second ahead of the shot and somersaulted on the ground. Terra followed.

"Stick together, sisters!" ordered Lillie. "Fight them like a team!"

Windi threw her rifle onto the roof and flew out the window, blowing up the winds and turning dusty Main Street into a gray cloud that surrounded Rhino Bill's wagon. He ran to escape the dust and was punched in the back of the head by a bolt of hard air from Windi.

"Bill!" shouted Annie. She lifted her rifle and shot Windi in the foot, forcing her to the ground.

"You stupid kid!" Windi cried. "You shot me."

Oceanna turned herself into moisture and rained out the window, completely covering the roof and streaming down through the gutters and into the street, where she sprayed Annie with a torrent of water that forced the rifle to slip out of her hand. Knocked to the ground, Annie started to swallow water and began to drown. Seeing this, Sheriff Earp stepped off the porch, pulled out his six-gun and fired a shot to distract Oceanna. She solidified, turned around, at which time he hit her with his fist, knocking her down.

Ginger then appeared behind him, the tips of her fingers on fire.

"Hit a woman, Sheriff?" she asked, pointing her flaming fingers at him and unleashing a torrent of burning fire that singed his hat, whiskers and shirtsleeves.

Terra followed Nikki down the street and lost her near the old post office. She walked around slowly, looking for Nikki, who had blended into the side of a barn in which the post office had been established years before. When Terra passed her, Nikki punched her in the jaw and then sent a strong undercut to her chest, and Terra went down to the ground.

Big mistake. In her element, Terra pounded the dirt with her fists, and the resulting tremor exploded with a bang that reverberated up and down Main Street, splitting it down the middle. The force knocked Rhino Bill into the gaping hole.

"Bill!" Annie yelled. But he had disappeared.

"Get up, sister," ordered Ginger, throwing her flames in an arc and keeping Earp at bay. Oceanna got up and exploded a wave out of her body that smacked Earp and knocked him hard to the ground. Then Annie picked up and fired her rifle and hit a hook that held up an old sign at the long-closed barbershop. It fell on Oceanna's head, knocking her out.

Down the street, Nikki jumped on Terra's back and pushed her face down in the dirt.

"You like dirt, lady?" she gritted out. "Here—eat your fill."

Nikki pounded Terra's head into the ground over and over again until she lost consciousness.

Rhino Bill had scaled the wall of the hole and was now climbing out.

"Kill him, Ginger!" Windi, said, holding her bleeding foot and sitting on the ground.

Unnoticed by the heroes and villains fighting in the street, Lillie left the saloon building via the back stairs and was met by a waiting covered carriage that took off the moment she stepped inside.

Ginger made a move. Bursting completely into flames, she flashed toward Rhino Bill, who picked up a piece of wood from the broken wagon and charged Ginger. Seemingly unaffected by her flames, he hit her multiple times, finally succeeding in knocking her out and, putting out her flames.

"Great job, Protectors!" said Nikki as she approached and surveyed the fallen Langtrees sisters.

"Teamwork," said Earp. "But it looks like the real Lillie got away."

"Probably to go after Holliday," said Nikki, helping Earp up. "You OK?"

"Yup," he said. "Except for my pride."

"Them girls did look a mite similar," said Annie.

"'Sisters,' I heard one of 'em say," said Rhino Bill.

"Clones," said Nikki. "They're clones."

All three Protectors looked at her blankly.

"Duplicates," said Nikki. "Doppelgangers. Body doubles."

"But they sure did wear some pretty dresses," said Annie.

"Hey, what about me?" yelled Windi. "I need a doctor."

CHAPTER EIGHTEEN

"Boss," said Ben, "you gotta cut it out. I mean, all the pacing. It's driving me crazy!"

"Be quiet," said Terry, the other bodyguard. "The boss is thinking."

In his suite at a fine hotel in Prairie Junction, Doc Holliday paced nervously back and forth, mumbling to himself about timing, the bomb, and Lillie. Then he abruptly stopped.

"Shut up, both of you!" snapped Holliday. "You're ruining my finest hour. The train carrying my enemy, the Leader Garfield, is on its way and will be here later in the day."

"Ah, the bomb" said Ben. "Where is it, boss?"

"It's over there in that large leather bag on the bed," Holliday said, pointing.

"You mean…it's in here—with us?" said Ben. "In this room?"

"I said, over there on the bed," Holliday said. "But don't you worry, you sniveling coward. The bomb is harmless without the detonation device, and I had that hidden in the desert, miles away from here."

"Whew," said Ben. He walked to the window.

"Boss, how you going to get that bomb on the train?" asked Terry.

"I have someone planted on the train," said Holliday.

"Like a spy?" asked Terry.

"Who's this guy on the inside, boss?" asked Ben.

"You idiots!" said Holliday. "It's Damian."

"Ah, why don't you just have Damian kill Garfield instead of the bomb, boss?" asked Terry.

"That wouldn't be any fun," said Holliday. "An exploding bomb makes a much bigger statement."

Having killed the real conductor before they left the station in New Canton, Damian took his place, posing as the conductor, and managed to pull it off, both men being bald and having a similar height and weight.

But he did not fool everyone.

Damian passed through Leader Garfield's office car and continued to walk into the next car, not noticing Garfield himself sitting at his desk.

Something's not right with that man, thought Garfield. Even though the man who'd just passed looked exactly like the other conductor, this one made him feel uneasy, somehow not safe. He told Lucretia afterwards about his suspicions, and she scolded him, but he told his security detail anyway. From that moment on, the new conductor was under observation if not outright suspicion. The Leader promised himself that this conductor would not be leaving Prairie Junction on his train.

The door opened, and Damian walked back into the car, this time noticing the Leader seated at his desk.

"Sir," he said, "is there anything I can get you?"

"Just the estimated time of our arrival in Prairie Junction," he said. "I need enough time to prepare my speech."

"Less than five hours before we arrive, sir," said Damian who checked his pocket watch.

"Thank you, conductor. Let me know when we arrive."

Lillie Langtrees's carriage headed east out of Ghost Town. She got as far as the desert before her horse-drawn carriage and driver came under attack from a four-foot-tall wooden contraption driven by a steam engine and modeled after a childhood pet—a dog. It came equipped with movable joints; sharp, rusted metal teeth for protection; a sturdy rhino-leather hide; and a fierce mechanical bark that scared people away.

Alex Bell had named the dog prototype Spot because of an acid spill that had caused multiple discolorations on its steam-driven metal heart. Lillie's carriage horse jumped and bolted, throwing the driver to the ground. Spot chased it as Lillie, trapped inside the careening carriage, screamed and was tossed around. Made mostly of wood, Spot sounded like a rickety fence on a windy day, but it managed to overtake the carriage and stop the runaway horse. Lillie landed on her butt when the impact forced open the carriage door and threw her to the ground.

Bell stepped out from behind a clump of tall cacti.

"Good boy," he said to the sitting Spot. "Just need to check a few things..."

Bell reached down, lifted off the top of Spot's head, and pulled out a small cylindrical plug. The wooden dog sat quietly, its connection broken. Bell then pulled a six-gun out of a holster and walked toward Lillie, who had not moved, possibly still in shock from what had just transpired.

"Get up, Miss Langtrees," Bell said, pointing the gun at her.

"What?" Lillie said, somewhat confused. "Who are you?"

"I'm Alex Bell," he said, "inventor and newest deputized member of the Protectors. I just happened to be out here testing my latest weapon when I saw your carriage fleeing Ghost Town. I'm sure you're up to no good, so I'm taking you back. You're under arrest for the crimes of prostitution, grand larceny, and trading in dead bodies."

She laughed.

"You've got no proof of *any* of that," said Lillie as she stood up. "Besides, I don't believe you'd shoot a woman."

"You're right," Bell said. "I would never shoot a woman, especially one as beautiful as you, Miss Langtrees. But if you don't surrender right now, I'll be forced to reactivate that almost-as-big-as-you wooden dog over there, and...well, its rusty teeth are pretty sharp."

"Papers!" shouted a bony boy of no more than seven selling newspapers on the corner at the Prairie Junction train station. "Get your papers here!"

A crowd of people gathered around him to read the headlines.

"Leader trades in combat boots for high-heeled shoes!" announced the paperboy for everyone to hear. "Get your papers!"

Most of the crowd was at the station awaiting the arrival of Leader Garfield, who, after arriving, would give a public speech from the back of his train before heading off to the western coast.

A loud, shrill whistle blew, accompanied by a cloak of cloudy steam released from the mighty engine that pulled into the station, announcing the arrival of Garfield's train. The crowd lunged toward the tracks as it came to a rest under the station's long copper roof.

First out of the train was the Leader's security detail. With rifles in hand, they checked every corner of the station before signaling an OK back to the train. The crowd grew louder as the back door opened, and Leader Garfield and his family stepped out. The crowd applauded. He waved to the gathered citizens, including the region's press, who wanted to meet him in person.

"Thank you!" said Leader Garfield. "Thank you for coming out today to greet me and my loving family. Lucretia, come take a bow."

She did so and then got back in line.

"I am humbled," he said.

More applause from the crowd.

"You know, sitting at my big desk in Washington, DC, I sometimes wonder what it's like for you, the ordinary citizens who live out here where the fertile prairie ends and the cool, sandy desert begins. Frankly, I'm envious, and so I said to my wife, 'Lucretia, we should go out to meet the little people who make up this great continent and ask them what our government could be doing better.' And she said, 'Why not take a trip?' And so, here we are with our new baby and our rambunctious twin boys."

Further applause and laughter came from the crowd.

"We need the army out here," yelled a woman standing about ten feet away from the Leader, "to protect us from them savages!"

"Our wells have run dry," said an older man in the back. "We need water, not introductions!"

"And more to eat," cried a short woman near the front row of people. "My babies go hungry every night of the week."

"Leader?" asked a reporter for a major politically opposed news outlet. "Is there any truth to the rumor that you like to dress up in women's clothes?"

Before Garfield could answer, two big security guards went over, picked the reporter up, and dragged him away.

"Ladies and gentlemen," the Leader said, "our nation is united—the most it's been in years. Now, I know we all have our little issues, but let me reassure you, my good people of..."

"Prairie Junction," prompted Lucretia.

"Prairie Junction," he said, "that trade with the other continents is keeping people employed, and the western territories have opened up to development that promises to rebalance the population and bring in new customers for your goods and services. Why, I just signed a law that will allow the indigenous populations to have a claim on their land."

There were rumblings among people in the crowd and then silence.

"Native lover!" someone shouted from the back.

"Go home!" yelled a sweet-looking old woman, and she spit on the ground.

A few others in the crowd booed the Leader, and his family closed in around them.

"My fellow Nenans!" shouted the Leader. "We cannot let our petty grievances stop us from making progress where it is needed the most."

"How is that fair?" asked a twentysomething male with long straight hair sticking out from under a roughed-up cap. "We have to pay, and they'll get theirs for free!"

"These troubled times," Garfield said, "demand sacrifice so that each and every one of us can be equal and so that we can help others less fortunate than ourselves to prosper. It's the right thing to do."

"Hypocrite!" yelled a woman in the front row. She threw her shoe at the Leader. "You're rich! It's easy for you to be so generous!"

A security guard quickly escorted her out as she continued shouting.

"I see we have some nonbelievers," said Garfield. "I implore you to give me time and the benefit of the doubt to make things right with you. Today I intend to have lunch with your mayor while my wife and children walk around this charming place you call Prairie Town. All except the baby—she'll be staying on the train to take her nap."

"Junction!" someone shouted back.

"What?" he asked. "Oh...yes. Prairie *Junction*."

More grumbling was heard from some in the crowd.

"My dear friends," said the Leader. "After I'm gone, think about what I've told you, and remember to help someone if you can. Thank you very much."

Tepid applause.

The Leader and his family walked back into the train, followed by his armed guards. Unnoticed by anyone on or around the train, Damian walked quickly past the other parked trains in the station's yard, and into a cornfield. There in the center stood a big, dilapidated barn with double-X painted doors. He knocked four times in a pattern, and slowly the large doors opened.

"Good, you're on time, Damian," said Doc Holliday as he stood inside the barn with Ben and Terry.

"Everything is going according to plan," Damian said. "I just need the package."

Terry was holding a very large leather bag.

"Give him the bag," said Holliday.

Terry walked over to where Damian stood and handed him the leather bag.

"I want the bomb placed in the baby's pram," said Holliday, "where it will do the maximum amount of damage."

"Kill a baby, boss?" asked Ben. "That's rough."

Holliday smiled at him. "You're lucky I can't shoot my gun in here without arousing suspicion so close to the Leader's train, or you'd have been dead a second after you said *baby*."

"Boss, I…" stammered Ben, stumbling backward out of the way.

Holliday reached down, pulled a very sharp knife from inside his boot, and held it up to the light. "But a knife will do just as good a job."

Holliday grabbed Ben by the neck, twisted him around, and cut a very deep gash into his face, one that would leave a lasting scar.

Ben used his hand to cover his bleeding face and staggered away from Holliday.

"You're lucky I need you," said Holliday. "Otherwise, I would have slit your throat and not your pretty face."

CHAPTER NINETEEN

The diminutive Lillie Langtrees paced back and forth in her Ghost Town jail cell like a cat locked in a public washroom.

"Sheriff!" she called from her cell. "I want to see my lawyer!"

"I'm sorry, Lillie," said Sheriff Wyatt Earp. "Your lawyer was found dead yesterday. Hanged himself."

"But that can't be," she said. "Holliday said he was to be trusted."

"Don't be a fool," said Earp. "Holliday trusts no one, including you. That's why you're stuck in this jailhouse with me and not out on the run with him—trust."

"Wyatt?" said Nikki Hale. "It's time to go."

Out in the office, Rhino Bill Cody, Annie Oakely, Alex G. Bell, and Chief Iron Weed waited.

"Bell's confirmed it, Sheriff," said Rhino Bill. "The target."

"Mind sharing that with the rest of us, Bell?" said the sheriff.

"Miss Langtrees told me under pressure," said Bell, "that Doc Holliday went up to Prairie Junction to meet a train that was carrying Leader Garfield, intending to blow it up with a bomb."

"How did you convince her to tell you, Alex?" asked Nikki.

"It took a bit of persuasion," said Alex. "And a little help from my latest invention: a fierce steam-powered dog."

"Great job, Alex," said Earp, extending his hand, "no matter how you got her confession. Welcome to the team."

"Prairie Junction," Annie said. "Why, that's only a couple of hours away, three at the most."

Lillie, overhearing the Protectors' conversation, sat down on her bunk and lowered her head.

"I think the four of us should ride up there together," Earp said. "Alex, you and Chief Iron Weed will stay here with his men to watch Lillie and take care of any trouble that may arise in Ghost Town."

"By the way," said Annie, "where'd her sisters get to?"

"Funny thing," said Earp. "When we locked them up after the fight, they all melted away. Left just smudge puddles behind."

"It was nasty," said Nikki. "Took a lot of scrubbing to wipe them away."

"You think you've won," said Lillie with a laugh from her cell. "But you've gained nothing, because Holliday thought it all through…and he left something to remember him by."

"What did he leave?" asked Earp, his tone serious.

"Buried bombs," she said.

"Did he tell you where he had them buried?" asked Nikki.

"I guess it doesn't matter now," said Lillie.

"Tell us what you know, Lillie," Earp said, "and I'll recommend that the judge go light on your sentence."

"Doc Holliday had his men bury explosives under Ghost Town," Lillie said. "He plans on detonating them right after he blows up the train."

"How's he going to do that from Prairie Junction?" asked Rhino Bill.

"Over the telewire," said Alex Bell. "I developed the trigger in Holliday's lab. I'm the one responsible for his being able to blow up Ghost Town from hours' distance away."

Damian boarded the train, the heavy leather bag holding a bomb in his hand. Unknown to him, he had been followed. One of Leader Garfield's security guards had trailed Damian on his rendezvous with Holliday at the barn where he'd picked up the bomb. The security guard was following the orders of Garfield, who wanted the conductor shadowed.

"Excuse me, Conductor," said a well-dressed elderly woman who'd boarded the train in Prairie Junction. "When will we be departing this station?"

"In exactly fifteen minutes, ma'am," the conductor said. "But I think you're on the wrong train."

"Oh, my," said the woman, puzzled. "I'd better get off before we depart."

"If you give me a minute to put down my bag," said the conductor, "I'll escort you off the train."

"That would be wonderful," she said. "I'll just wait right here."

Damian exited the car carrying the leather bag and made his way into the office car and then to the next car, that was the Garfield family quarters. He knocked on the small glass window on the car's door. The children's nanny appeared on the opposite side of the glass and then opened the door.

"The missus needs you to bring her gray shawl," said Damian. "Out on the platform."

"Why can't you bring it to her?" asked the nanny.

"I have to get the train ready to depart this station," he said. "I don't have time to run your errands."

"Very well," she said, "but you'll have to watch the baby."

"No problem."

"I'll be back in a moment."

The nanny picked up Mrs. Garfield's shawl and walked out the rear of the railroad car. As soon as she was gone, Damian, still carrying the bomb in a leather bag, walked over to the baby's pram and looked inside. Garfield's baby girl, Louise, was sleeping soundly.

Opening the bag, Damian pulled out a device that looked like a large windup clock with four sticks of dynamite secured by braided hemp cord. The bomb was about the size of a small rooster and had wires on the top and bottom and a blinking device on the face of the clock that counted down the seconds. With more hemp cord he found in the bag, Damian tied the bomb under the pram, above the wheels and hidden behind a large, folded pink blanket. He stood up and looked again into the pram. The baby was wide wake at this point and staring up at him. Then she smiled.

Leader Garfield thanked Prairie Junction's mayor and his staff for their hospitality and bid farewell from the train station to a somewhat smaller crowd than earlier in the day. It was just before sunset and nightfall began to cover the eastern sky and temperatures began to cool across the vast desert. The plan was for the Leader and his family to sleep on the train that night and wake up in the morning out west in the desert and go on to the coast.

"My family and I would like to thank you again," said the Leader. "You fine citizens of Prairie Junction, you have a great little community here... and an even brighter tomorrow."

There was mild applause from the assembled people, mostly older women and kids, some of whom were already walking away as the Leader waved his hat farewell.

"All aboard," called the conductor.

Garfield and his family entered the train, followed by the security detail, and then Damian closed the door. The shrill steam whistle blew, and the Leader's private train pulled out of the station and headed west toward the coast, traveling by night to avoid the scorching heat of day and the unwanted attention from any local politicians who may have reason to harm the progressive Leader Garfield.

CHAPTER TWENTY

The Protectors arrived in Prairie Junction around sunset on horseback. They headed for the train station at a fast clip, but Main Street in Prairie Junction was crowded with horseback riders, wagons, and vendor carts. Sporadically along the way, children would run out into the street and try to spook the horses until their parents threatened them back into the shadows.

"Protectors," said Sheriff Wyatt Earp, "the train station is just up ahead."

They galloped through town and arrived at the train station with its three tracks and two parked trains. The Leader's train had just pulled out.

"We missed it," said Rhino Bill Cody.

"I can still see it in the distance," said Annie Oakley, pulling her rifle out of its sheath.

The lights on the back of the train were just disappearing into the dark night's sky.

"If Holliday has made good on his promise to kill Leader Garfield," said Nikki Hale, "then he must be here and staying in one of the hotels. Maybe we can catch him before he has time to detonate his bomb."

"Let's check the hotels," said Rhino Bill, "before the scum gets away."

"You three go ahead," said Earp. "I'll go after the Leader's train. Maybe

I can catch it."

"The steam engine is faster than a horse, Sheriff," said Rhino Bill.

"I gotta try," said Earp. He turned his horse and followed the departing train out into the increasingly black star-filled night.

"Wyatt!" cried Nikki. "Wait!"

Nikki rode over to where Earp had stopped.

"I just wanted to say that…I…" Nikki stumbled in her speech. "I… care about you Wyatt…a lot."

"I feel the same way, Nikki," he said. "But we got a job to do. We're Protectors now."

"You're right," she laughed and reached over her horse, and he met her halfway. They kissed passionately for several moments until…

"Best get after that train, Sheriff," said Rhino Bill. "It's getting away."

Nikki watched Earp leave on horseback and couldn't help but think it might be the last time she'd ever see him. Maybe he'd never return, or maybe she'd just disappear into thin air the way she'd initially arrived to this time and place. She didn't belong here, and the longer she stayed, the harder it would be to leave—especially now that she had expressed her feelings for Earp.

"Nikki," asked Annie. "You OK?"

Moments after the train left the station, after a brief struggle between the railroad cars, Damian had stabbed to death the security guard who had been following him on Garfield's orders and pushed the dead guard's body off the train.

Moving to the front of the train, he knocked on the glass in the engine car, and the engineer waved him in.

"Any trouble tonight?" Damian asked the engineer who stood at the controls, basically, two tall levers protruding out of the floor, one to accelerate, and the other to brake the train.

"Nope," he said. "Been quiet so far."

"Good," said Damian, and without further ado, he used both his strong hands to strangle the engineer, squeezing the last breath out of him. Then he used hemp cord from his pocket to tie the dead engineer to the train's brake and leaned him forward. The corpse's weight on the brake would keep the train in motion, but slow it down as it approached the spot where Doc Holliday waited in ambush. Once the engineer was secured, Damian walked out of the engine car and back into the main body of the train, passing Leader Garfield's security contingent who noticed the train had begun to slow down and were on high alert.

"We think there's an intruder on the train," one of them said.

Another yelled, "Move!"

"An intruder?" Damian said. "That would be me."

Before the guards had a chance to react, Damian moved quickly with his sharp knife in hand and cut the guards deeply along their necks and shoulders. Then he stabbed one and gutted the other, stepped over the bodies, and moved on. Arriving at the Leader's office car, he stopped, noticing another security guard stationed in front of the door. He shifted the sharp, bloodied knife behind his back before moving forward.

"I have an important message for the Leader," said Damian.

"Yeah?" replied the female guard. "Tell me what it is."

"Sorry," said Damian. "I can tell only the Leader himself."

"Orders are that no one's allow in," said the guard. "But I'll ask him if he wants to see you."

"Thanks," said Damian, and when the security guard turned to open the door, Damian grabbed her by the collar, reached over quickly, and cut her throat, splattering blood everywhere and making the platform between cars very slippery.

Damian stepped over the still-bleeding body and walked into

Garfield's office car.

"Hey, Frankie," a security man called out, entering from the other end of the car. "You in here? Frankie?"

The guard stepped in, closed the door behind him, and walked slowly toward Garfield's empty desk.

"Frankie?"

Damian, already hiding inside, came up behind him and stuck his long knife into the security guard's back, twisting to make sure he cut through the rib cage cartilage and reached the man's beating heart.

Then the door flew open.

"What is going on in here?" demanded Leader Garfield. He walked into the office car and quickly observed that Damian was holding a man with a knife in his back and in a panic rushed forward out the door, tripping over the dead female guard's body and landing on his back between cars.

Damian pulled the knife out of the body he held and followed the Leader out, his sharp knife drawn in front of him. He hadn't been asked to kill Garfield by hand, but he wasn't about to stop himself. Holliday, he assumed, would be forever in his debt.

"An old acquaintance wants you dead, Leader," said Damian as he stood over the fallen Garfield, his hand holding the knife raised, poised to be plunged into Garfield's chest and heart.

Bam!

A shot fired from above hit Damian in the arm, forcing him to drop his knife.

It was Sheriff Wyatt Earp.

"You're under arrest," he said, swooping down from the train's roof.

Garfield crawled out of the way.

Damian tried to fight back, but his wound was substantial, and he wasn't able to put up much of a struggle. However, he wasn't ready to give up. He took a swing at Earp and hit him in the jaw. Unfazed, Earp swung back and knocked Damian into the closed car door, where he slid to the platform, defeated.

"You don't understand," said Damian. "We need to get off this train."

"Why is it slowing down?" Earp asked.

"To give the boss time to get into position," said Damian.

"Sir," Earp said to Garfield, "we believe a bomb has been planted on this train."

Leader Garfield managed to stand.

"I'm aware this charlatan was up to no good," said Garfield. "And now my suspicions have been confirmed."

"Doesn't matter," Earp said. "We need to get you and your family off this train—*now*!"

"The train is moving too fast," said Garfield. "How can we?"

"It's slowing down," said Earp. "That's how I was able to catch up on horseback."

"Very brave," said Garfield.

"When the train slows down enough," said Earp, "jump off with your family."

"And what is your name, young man?" Garfield asked.

"Sheriff Wyatt Earp, sir," he said. "I'm with the Protectors, and we're at your service."

Rhino Bill Cody sat on his horse atop a hill just outside Prairie Junction and whistled into the wind.

Then he listened.

"Bill," said Annie Oakley, "you think this will work?"

"It'd better," Rhino Bill said. "Otherwise we're lost."

He whistled again.

"Bill," said Nikki Hale. "We shouldn't be sitting here—"

Hoot, hoot, hoo-hoo-oot! came back on the wind.

A large gray night owl with dark, shiny feathers flew out of a big oak tree nearby and landed on Rhino Bill's outstretched arm. It twisted its head all the way around, looking back toward the desert.

Hoo-oot, hoo-oot! Hoot!

"What's it saying, Bill?" asked Annie.

"Uncle Owl says there's a shortcut through the foothills we can take to meet up with the train on the other side."

"Animals are pretty smart," said Annie. "Not like some people."

"No disrespect to Uncle Owl, Bill," said Nikki, "but I'll bet the steam train carrying Garfield and his family is long gone."

Hoot! Hoo-oot! The owl flapped its wings. *Hoot! Hoot!*

"Mite riled up," said Annie.

"He said the train has slowed down about two miles out of town," said Rhino Bill.

"That's not far," said Annie.

"Well, I guess we'll have to trust what the bird is telling you, Bill," said Nikki. "And follow his advice."

"Uncle," said Rhino Bill. "Show us the way."

The owl flew up into the night sky, off toward the southwest, and with the help of the full moonlight, the Protectors followed.

"This spot is perfect," said Doc Holliday earlier in the day as he stood on the railroad tracks a few miles outside Prairie Junction. "I can easily detonate my bomb from here."

"If the bomb is so long distance, boss," said Ben, a large bandage covering one side of his face, "then how come we can't move farther away from the train?"

"The bomb has its range limits," said Holliday. "Bell built it in a hurry, and on my orders he may have had to cut corners. So the distance between where we need to stand and the bomb is not what I anticipated, but it's one that I accept. Why? Do you have a problem with that?"

"Uh...yeah—no, boss," said Ben. "I mean, no. Of course, no."

"Then get to work! Knock down those pine trees and place them on the train track in the exact spot I indicated—and do it quick."

"Is that why you had us bring them saws, boss?" asked Ben.

"Just do it," bellowed Holliday, pulling out his six-gun and cocking the trigger. "Or do you want me to blow off the other half of your face?"

"OK, boss," said Terry. "We'll get right to it. Ben didn't mean no disrespect."

Under Holliday's watchful eye, the two burly bodyguards cut down several eight-foot desert pine trees and carried them to the railroad tracks, where they placed them in a pile. The obstacle would not be seen after dark.

"If you got a bomb, boss," said Ben, "then why the trees?"

"Insurance," said Holliday. "In case Bell double-crossed me and his bomb turns out to be a dud."

"Boss?"

"I'm sick of your questions!"

"Sorry, boss," said Ben. "But could we—"

"Finish up," said Holliday, "and go meet my enemy's train. I'll wait here."

The two bodyguards rode off, and Doc Holliday watched the sunset.

"Revenge is at hand," he whispered to himself. "The man responsible for my family's collapse, the evil banker Garfield, along with his entire family will be blown to bits. Then I will finally be at peace."

CHAPTER TWENTY-ONE

The Leader's train barreled through the dark desert night, albeit at a much slower speed than before the engineer was murdered and his body tied to the falling brake. It was still going fast enough, though, to make it dangerous to jump off.

"Can't we disarm the bomb?" asked Leader Garfield.

"We don't have the time to look for it, Leader," said Sheriff Wyatt Earp. "Better if you get off this train."

"I need to get my family," Garfield said.

"Where are your guards?" asked Earp, looking around the platform.

"All dead, I assume," said the Leader. "The conductor must have killed them all."

"I'd better check on the engineer," said Earp. "You get your family, sir, and meet me back here as soon as you can."

"Can't we wait until the train stops, Sheriff?" asked Earp. "And then all get off?"

"We can't take that chance," said Earp. "I think whatever is about to happen will happen very soon."

Garfield stepped off the platform and headed to the sleeper car, where his family was gathered, intent on getting them off the train.

"Please," he cried out to Lucretia. "We have to hurry!"

"Poppa?" asked the twins in unison. "What's happening?"

Chaos ensued as they scrambled to grab their belongings in the crowded train car, not understanding they had no time to waste.

"Leave your things!" ordered Garfield. "We have to go now."

"Go where?" asked Lucretia. "The train is moving, James! There's no place for us to go."

"We have to be ready, Lu," he said. "Now, grab a child and follow me."

The nanny lifted Louise from the pram while Lucretia gathered the twin boys and marched them toward the door. Garfield waited for the nanny and his daughter by the door, and as they passed, he escorted them out and onto the platform and into the next car.

Damian regained enough of his strength to retreat back into the office car, smashing everything in his way.

"Conductor!" shouted Sheriff Earp, who noticed he was missing and followed him. "There's no place to hide! Give yourself up to the strong arm of the law."

"I'm getting off this train, Sheriff," said Damian from behind an overturned rhino-hide sofa. "And you're not going to stop me."

Damian made his move toward the door between railroad cars, and Earp ran to catch him.

"No, you don't," said Earp. He threw a punch, but Damian was able to duck. Damian, still bleeding from the gunshot wound, punched Earp in the stomach and the jaw, knocking him to the floor.

"Big man sheriff," said Damian, stepping on the fallen Earp with his boot. He then reached over and grabbed the cord of a broken lamp, wrapping it around Earp's neck and cutting off his air supply. Earp's face turned almost blue.

"Can't...breathe!"

"Good-bye, lawman," said Damian. "Long live the Resurrectionists!"

When Damian looked up to utter those words, Earp suddenly grabbed and twisted his boot, using it as leverage to get Damian off him, and then wrapped both his legs around Damian's, forcing him to the floor. Now free, Earp jumped up, grabbed Damian by the collar, and dragged him out of the railroad car to the edge of the platform. With a strong kick, he pushed him off the train, down to the desert floor below, where Damian landed with a thud and rolled unconscious to a stop in the cool darkness.

Doc Holliday's two bodyguards, Ben and Terry, reached the Leader's train at about the same time the Protectors arrived there from Prairie Junction. A confrontation was inevitable. They split up, Ben going to the front of the train and Terry to the back, where he immediately fired on the approaching Rhino Bill Cody and missed. Without warning, Annie Oakley returned fire but missed when he moved.

Ben rode his horse up on the moving train and looked through the window of the car in which Garfield and his family were waiting for Earp to return. Holding his horse at a gallop, Ben pulled out a six-gun and fired through the window glass, missing Garfield and killing the nanny, who dropped the baby and fell dead in front of the twins. Rhino Bill, also heading to the front of the train, saw his chance and pulled out his lasso, spinning it in the air as he approached Ben. Quietly in position, Rhino Bill threw his spinning lasso out into the dark night air and successfully landed it over

Ben's head. As he fought, Rhino Bill tugged, pulling Ben off his horse and dragging him several feet over the desert sand, tearing his bandage and reopening his deep facial wound.

The other bodyguard, Terry, was approaching the moving train on horseback, ready to jump from his horse onto a platform between the cars, when a shot rang out from Annie's rifle. Hit in the shoulder, Terry fell to the ground and rolled into a ditch.

Sheriff Wyatt Earp made his way to the front of the train and peered through the engineer's cabin window. He could see the engineer—he was not moving. Earp forced his way in and discovered the engineer tied to the brake, slowly forcing the train to slow down. He grabbed the engineer's body and tried to lift it off the brake, but the man was too heavy. Trying another tack, Earp pushed the man forward, forcing the brake to the floor, but the engineer's leg was caught underneath him, so the brake could not fully depress to stop the train.

Then a rifle shot rang out, and Earp knew he had to hurry.

Nikki Hale pulled her horse close to the rear of the moving train and stood up in the saddle, steadying her balance in order to execute a double flip onto the platform. With a soft grunt, she landed on her feet between the office and sleeping cars within view of the Leader and his family, who were huddled together in the office car. They just stared at her.

"Don't be afraid of me," Nikki called out when she got inside. "I'm here to rescue you."

The nanny lay dead, bleeding out on the floor. Lucretia and her two boys ran to Nikki while Leader Garfield stayed behind his overturned wooden desk, holding his infant daughter who he'd picked up from the fallen nanny's arms. She was fast asleep.

"Hurry, everyone," said Nikki. "The train has slowed down enough to safely get you off."

Nikki and Lucretia, followed by the boys, walked out of the car and onto the platform while Garfield moved toward the door, his baby in hand.

"I'm going to need you to be brave," said Nikki to the young twin boys. "You're going to ride on the horse, and Mommy will follow right behind you, OK?"

The twins shook their heads.

Then Rhino Bill and Annie galloped up and rode parallel with the train. Nikki nudged the twins closer.

"Don't be afraid!" Lucretia called out. "I'll be right behind you."

Rhino Bill reached out and grabbed one twin and Annie the other, whom they swung up behind them in the saddle, still keeping pace with the train.

"Come on!" Rhino Bill called out. "Jump!"

As Lucretia hesitated, Annie rode off with one young twin.

"I can't!" Lucretia said. "I'm afraid!"

"Don't be," said Nikki. "The Protectors have got your back."

With that, Nikki pushed, Rhino Bill pulled, and Lucretia was off the train and onto Rhino Bill's horse, where she clung until he slowed and dropped her safely onto the ground.

"My husband and baby!" Lucretia cried out. "They are still on the train!"

Doc Holliday saw the train lights approaching from miles away. He was excited. It was time. He picked up the detonation device created by Alex Bell—based on his telewire expertise, which promised to eliminate the need for short-term fuses and close encounters with unstable explosives—and placed it in his lap, fiddling with the knobs, exposed wires, and curved copper conductors that took up most of the space on the top end of the rectangular object.

The approaching train's headlights grew stronger.

"Where are those two idiots?" he asked, irritably. "They were supposed to warn me."

The soft, sandy ground beneath Holliday's feet began to rubble as the mighty steam engine drew near, and he could hear a squealing sound, like a herd of hogs at feeding time, increase in volume.

"Wait..." he told himself as the wind picked up. "Let the train pass before you press the button."

The steam train had slowed, its brake engaged, but still continued to move.

"Three...two...one..." he counted down out loud. "Boom."

Holliday pressed the big red button in the middle of the detonation device's panel and braced for an explosion. The train passed with its brakes squealing and smoking, but nothing else happened until it rammed the cut pine trees piled up on the track. Not carrying enough force to break through, the train bounced to a halt with a jolt.

"Son of a gun!" Holliday yelled, stomping around and pointing to the sky. "I am going to kill that Bell!"

"You need to get off this train, sir," said Nikki as she reentered the office car.

"Please, follow me out."

"You and your friends saved my wife and sons," said Garfield, holding his baby girl near the door. "For that, I am eternally grateful."

Garfield handed the infant girl to Nikki, who grabbed her and held her tightly. Then she extended her hand to the Leader.

Moments later, Rhino Bill and Annie arrived, along with Leader Garfield's wife and twins.

"My baby!" Lucretia said. "Where is my baby girl?"

"She's here with me," said Nikki, who appeared holding the infant, Louise. "And she's all right."

Relieved, Lucretia ran to Nikki and picked up her baby daughter.

The boys looked around. "Poppa?" they asked.

"I'm here," said Garfield, stepping down from the train. He had a minor gash on this forehead caused by the moving train's abrupt stop.

The twins ran to their father's arms.

"Everybody looks OK," said Rhino Bill from atop his horse.

"We got lucky," said Nikki. "The bomb didn't detonate and blow up the train."

"Oh, I wouldn't say you were so lucky," said Doc Holliday, who stepped out of the dark brush beyond the tracks holding a loaded six-gun pointed at Garfield. "I'm still alive, and I intend to kill the man who ruined my family."

"I think you are mistaken, sir," said Garfield.

"Mistaken?" said Holliday. "You foreclosed on my family, and now I'm here today to avenge my dead."

"That was a long time ago," said Garfield. "But I am sorry for your loss."

"Too late," said Holliday, cocking back the trigger of his pistol and firing three shots that flashed white in the dark desert landscape.

All anyone saw was a flash of the red sash against the moonlight as Nikki jumped in front of Leader Garfield and took the three bullets full force into her body before crashing to the ground. She died within seconds.

"Stupid girl," said Holliday, raising his gun to fire again. "Don't anyone move. I have more bullets."

Bam!

The gunshot rang out from the front of the train, and the flash revealed it had come from Sheriff Earp's gun. Doc Holliday dropped his six-gun, which hit the ground before his body did, a look of shock on his face as he fell. Earp staggered toward Nikki's body. The others gathered around.

"I hit my head when the train bounced," mumbled Earp. Slowly, he picked Nikki's body up in his arms and held her close to his chest. "I was too late to save her," he cried.

"I'm sorry, Sheriff," said Leader Garfield. "She saved me and my family. Again, I'm very sorry."

"It all happened so fast," said Annie. "But we should have been faster."

Rhino Bill was too choked up to speak.

The baby began to cry.

"Nikki! Come *back*!"

"Nikki's gone, my friend," said Rhino Bill, quietly.

"She was the bravest of us all," said Annie.

"She was," said a twice broken-hearted Earp, still holding the dead Nikki in his arms. He looked west toward the mountains so they wouldn't see the tears in his eyes.

"Are you OK?" Garfield asked.

"I remember now," said Earp, "what Nikki was trying to tell me."

"What?" Rhino Bill asked.

"She said that in the future, where she came from, we were both part of a team, and we helped people. We saved lives together every day."

"The future?" said Annie in amazement. "What's the future like, Sheriff?"

"I don't know, Annie," Earp said, "but it must be wondrous."

THE END

Bonus Story

MEDIEVAL

Once upon a time, there lived a beautiful young queen by the name of Niz who ruled over a far-flung kingdom that extended from the eastern mountains on the Siberian coast to the thick western forests, where it was rumored evil elves and crafty witches practiced their dark arts in secret. Queen Niz had the respect of her people because she welcomed diversity and maintained the peace by continually traveling far and wide to visit distant relatives who were local advocates among her people.

Because of her popularity, Queen Niz was the envy of her peers. But it also made her a target—certain people wanted her removed. One day, the eighteen-year-old queen and her entourage, while traveling under snowy skies back to the capital from a relative's wedding, unknowingly crossed the property line of her evil cousin, an earth elemental by birth with a sour disposition who called himself Peter the Grimm.

The queen had heard rumors about her cousin's cruelty from her parents and members of her court and had hoped their paths would never cross, but that all changed when her carriage crossed the borderline.

Worse, Grimm knew she had trespassed and had already released his Dark Brigade guard to ambush her caravan.

"Oh, this has been a long day," said the queen as she reclined on animal fur blankets. Her six-foot-tall frame was covered in a green silk frock with low bodice that was belted at the waist. "I want to go home and sleep in my own bed."

"Yes, mum," said her maid, Lucy, a shy brunette with dimples on her cheeks. "But I don't like the look of this weather, mum. Too dark, it is, a bad omen."

"The dark can be comforting," said the queen.

"Some say this land belongs to your cousin, Peter the Grimm," said Lucy. "That we trespass."

"Nonsense," said Lord Boulderall, sipping his cup of wine. "These lands we cross belong to the queen and not some fool who challenges the throne."

"Leave her be," said Nanny, the fourth in the carriage. "I too worry we may encounter evil forces."

The journey was long and the weather damp. The carriage bounced and shook on the pitted, muddy roads, and the queen spent her time trying to read royal decrees and signing her wishes into law.

"When will we be home, Boulderall?" asked the queen.

"We still have miles more to go, Your Majesty," he said.

"I don't like the looks of this place," said the middle-aged nanny as she peered out the carriage window. "Like death itself out there—neither trees, green grass, nor any signs of life."

"Close the window, Nanny," said the queen. "It's better not to look."

Outside was a dark, uneven, broken place where nothing grew. The winds howled constantly and pushed against the rocks, warning that anyone foolish enough to travel these grim lands had better beware their surroundings.

Queen Niz longed to be back home with her family, and friends. She lived in a magnificent palace heated by a deep-pitted volcano that lay under her castle.

"Perhaps I should speak with the driver," said the queen. "Maybe there's a shortcut we can travel and make better time."

"My queen!" shouted the nanny. "Be careful! Speaking to the lesser born could hurt your vocabulary."

"Silly Nanny," said the queen. "Be still."

Queen Niz lowered her window and leaned out of her carriage.

"Driver," she called, "how soon before we are out of this wretched place?"

Manned by two drivers who wore heavy rain gear, the golden carriage was followed by two mounted guards and three other carriages for the servants and luggage that bought up the rear.

The older driver on the left handed the horses' reins to the other driver and turned around to respond to the young queen.

"Yes, Majesty?" he asked. "How can I help?"

"How soon will we be clear of this road?" she asked. "I mean, is there a shortcut back to the capital?"

"Sorry, Your Highness," he said. "We still have a long way to go. Of course, there is a detour up head, about two miles from here. If you'd like, we could take the detour. It may save us a full hour's travel."

"Yes," she said. "We will do that."

"It could be dangerous, Majesty," said the younger driver, still holding the reins. "Peter the Grimm is a murderer!"

"Hold your tongue, boy!" the older driver warned. "The queen is not to be questioned."

"Outrageous," said Lord Boulderall, who drank more wine.

The older driver took back the reins and signaled the two mounted riders behind the carriage that he was about to change course. The team of six large, strong horses swung to the right, heading toward twin Siberian mountains and Dead Man's Pass, the gateway to the red valley, the capital, and home.

Queen Niz sat back down on her seat and adjusted her thick, upswept ocean-blue hair. A natural beauty, she did not dwell on her looks but rather focused on education and the occult.

"Are you all right, Your Highness?" asked Nanny.

"Just a little tired," she said, "and getting anxious for home."

"Yes," Nanny said. "Everything will be all right when we're back home."

"I'm worried my cousin Peter will try to stop us," said the queen. "Although we've never met, my father once told me a story about his evil nature and his appropriation of his neighbor's kingdom. Our family even went to battle against his, but that was before I was born, when they tried to take our lands."

"I'm not one to gossip," said the nanny in a low voice, "but they say Peter the Grimm keeps the skulls of his victims lined up along the wall like they was trophies."

"Well, it's a good thing our driver knows a shortcut, then," Queen Niz said with a smile. "I'm sure we'll be home in no time."

"Watch out!" screamed the young driver as the lead horses on the queen's carriage tripped over a twisted rope that had been pulled across the road at Dead Man's Pass.

This caused a domino effect, dragging the other horses and the carriage itself down with them into a ditch. Everything tumbled and rolled, killing all the horses when they impacted en masse with a very large rock. The carriage cracked open like an egg into two almost complete halves. Nanny was ejected, hitting her head on a stump on her descent. Lord Boulderall was thrown into the air and broke his neck when he hit the ground. Lucy bounced and was impaled after landing on the carriage's broken axle. Both drivers, older and younger, were thrown from the carriage's top seat and landed in soft, marshy soil, cushioning their fall. Queen Niz was propelled backward into the air and landed on one of the broken halves of the carriage, her impact cushioned by the soft, plush furs she clutched to her side.

The two mounted guards arrived at the ditch and were killed by flying arrows before they could even dismount.

On top of the nearby ridge appeared the Dark Brigade, five of them on horseback. Two carried bows. They rode down and killed the rest of the servants and guards in the queen's caravan with arrows and spears. They then surrounded the broken carriage half that held the fallen queen.

"Pick up the queen," ordered one of the robed men clad all in black.

Another man dismounted, pulled the unconscious queen from the broken carriage, and lifted her up and over his saddle. Then the man who'd given the order noticed the drivers lying on the ground, momentarily in shock.

Someone moaned.

"They're still alive," said another man. He rode to where the sound emanated from and, with his sharpened spear with its large, pointed stone tip, struck the older driver in the head, forcing out his brain and killing him instantly. The younger driver tried to run away but was struck in the back by at least four sharp stone-tipped arrows. He fell to the ground, still alive, and tried to crawl away a few feet. But the man with the spear stabbed him through the heart, and he died as well.

Finished at the carriage's crash site, the Dark Brigade rode away with their prisoner as the swirling snow covered their tracks as well as all the dead bodies they left behind.

When word of the ambush reached the queen's father, Oman, regent of Siberia, he knew he had to get his daughter back as quickly as possible because his nephew, Peter the Grimm, was a sadist who tortured people for pleasure and revenge. He considered calling out the queen's army, but the majority of its ranks were too young and inexperienced to take on Grimm's fortified castle and the Dark Brigade, let alone cross desolate terrain that offered little camouflage. Oman realized he had no time to waste on amateurs—he needed professionals to rescue his daughter and remove the evil Grimm once and for all.

"Find me the ones they call the Protectors," said Oman. "I have use of their skills."

"As you wish, Majesty," said Drell, the senior diplomat.

Through his vast network of contacts, Drell found some people who knew where these Protectors might be found, but two separate attempts to do so met with failure. The Protectors were known to guard the innocent and subdue the criminal element—and they were masters at clandestine operations that kept them out of the public's eye.

On the third and final attempt, Drell sent a communiqué by carrier raven, begging them to intervene and save Queen Niz, before she could be deflowered—or worse.

"And after the queen is safely back in her own kingdom," wrote Drell, "you are personally asked by her father, Oman, regent of Siberia, to subdue and execute the evil Peter Grimm in the most egregious fashion so that his kingdom will go fallow, his body left to rot and his bones blasted by the howling, whipped-up sands to strip his corpse clean."

The response back came quickly, hand delivered by Ariel, the six-foot-six winged humanoid from the planet Aviana who flew into Oman's palace personally to deliver the group's message.

"We will return your queen to her rightful throne," said Ariel in a generic voice, neither female nor male. "And we do it for the good of the kingdom, not to assuage your personal grievances."

"I accept your help," said Oman, and he bowed to Ariel, who had landed on the palace floor and folded her wings, towering over Oman.

"Then we will be in touch," said Ariel. Spreading her wings once more, she lifted into the air and passed through the roof's open skylight, flying to the Protectors' headquarters hidden in the tall trees in the western forests of Siberia. Led by the swarthy, swashbuckling Romeo, this team of Protectors included Ariel, the winged warrior; Wave, an elemental who controlled the movement of water; and Spirit, an ethereal sorceress who cast spells and influenced minds at her will.

Queen Niz slowly opened her eyes. The place in which she was imprisoned was not familiar, and the smell was less than human. Her body was wrapped in a dirty tunic, and she was chained to a damp, cracked wall in a darkened room lit only by the glow of volcanic activity miles below the quartz floor.

Then she heard the moaning. Turning her head to the left and then the right, she soon realized she was not alone. Other men, women, and children of all ages, in various stages of dying, were also chained to the long walls. One man, his stomach organs ripped out, clung to life, but barely. The smell of rotting flesh and gallons of spilled blood was overwhelmingly bad. Against the far wall, she saw row after row of human skulls, stacked on top of one another.

"Cousin Niz."

A young man of about twenty-five stood before her. He wore ripped black tights and a bloodstained white tunic, which contrasted sharply with his mop of long curly black hair, soft-brown eyes, and warm, winning smile.

"I hope you haven't been too inconvenienced," he said, smirking.

"I'm chained to a wall," said the queen. "Why am I here? You surely don't want to start a war between our kingdoms. Now, let me go."

"I give the orders here, Your Highness," said Grimm. "Not you."

"Why have you imprisoned all these people here, Peter?" she asked. "What have you done?"

"These people are my...guests," he said with a smile. "Unfortunately, they have all outstayed their welcome."

The moans in the room got louder, and Peter the Grimm laughed. Then he snapped.

"Be quiet!" he demanded, "or I'll feed you to my dragons."

The moans quickly died down, and the man whose guts had fallen to the floor died.

"Bring her in," said Grimm to a tall, muscular Dark Brigade guard who stood by the door.

The guard left and shortly returned, dragging a young woman behind him. She was naked except for a dirty loincloth wrapped around her midsection.

"It's important that you understand who you are dealing with, dear Cousin," said Grimm.

"I think you a madman, Peter," said Queen Niz. "Let the girl go."

Grimm walked over to his wooden throne and sat down.

"Throw her in," Grimm said.

The Dark Brigade guard dragged the young woman to the edge of a bubbling, boiling tar pit and lifted her up. She let loose a blood-curdling scream and pounded his chest before he flung her into the boiling-hot tar, where she smoldered and burned all night long.

"I'm circling high above Grimm's fortress," relayed Ariel clairvoyantly through Spirit, the sorceress. "And I may have found the queen."

Ariel's reconnaissance mission above the castle was to locate any sign of Queen Niz. She circled again and again unnoticed, observing shifting guard patterns, the location of the prison in the castle, and food being delivered, indicating the queen may still be alive. Leaving Peter the Grimm's castle behind, Ariel flew back to the Protectors' headquarters, landing in their well-fortified tree house, where her teammates met and planned the rescue of the queen.

"I believe the queen to be alive," said Ariel, removing her golden helmet, "but I did not actually see her."

"We need more proof," said Romeo, current leader of the medieval Protectors.

"What's more, I believe she is being held in the prison tower where Grimm tortures his victims and displays their remains as trophies," said Ariel. "If she is alive and still in there, we need to rescue her—now!"

"We need to save the queen!" said Wave, a relative newcomer to the team who stood four and a half feet tall, wearing a deep blue vest over tights, and was able to transmute his body into liquid form. "But how can we get there? I don't fly."

"Before we overreact," said the ethereal Spirit, a silver-haired sorceress who wore a long white tunic and floated inches off the ground, "a little patience may be in order."

"What are you feeling, Spirit?" asked Romeo.

"My magic cannot cross the threshold to Grimm's castle," she said. "He must be collaborating with a demon from the netherworld that can shield him from my clairvoyant's probe."

"I can carry Wave," said Ariel. "He's small."

"Hey, birdy," said Wave. "It must get lonely way up there with your head in the clouds."

"Settle down," said Romeo. He wore maroon tights with a white blousy shirt over them and carried a sword in a scabbard around his trim waist. "But I agree—if the queen is being held in Grimm's castle, we must rescue her before it's too late."

"So, how do we get in?" asked Wave.

"That's where you come in, my young friend," said Romeo. "Ariel will fly you over the castle and drop you in the moat near the drawbridge, where you'll find a way into the castle and lower the drawbridge to let us in. When we locate the queen, Spirit will relay her location, and we'll meet up there."

"Sounds dangerous," said Wave. "But I'll do it."

"I'm going to enjoy this," said Ariel.

"I'll cast a spell of bravery over us," said Spirit, "to build up our resolve in the face of adversity."

"Thank you, Spirit," said Romeo. "But I'm not sure magic will help that which normally comes from within."

"How long will it take?" asked Ariel.

"What?" Wave asked.

"Spirit's spell," said Ariel. "How long will—"

"It's done," said Spirit.

"To save the queen," said Romeo. He raised his sword. "Protectors united!"

Ariel leaped off the tree house roof and flew into the clear afternoon sky.

"Are you sure this will work?" asked Wave as he stood on the edge of the roof.

"Let's hope so," Romeo said. "Now, get going, Wave, we'll be right behind you on horseback."

Ariel swooped down, fully spreading her almost-nine-foot wingspan, and picked Wave up in her strong arms, lifting him up and into the air.

Wave screamed as they descended twenty feet and then climbed skyward, the sound soon fading as they disappeared.

"Do you think they'll make it?" asked Spirit.

"You're the clairvoyant," Romeo said. "You tell me."

"Where are you going to drop me?" asked Wave, squirming in Ariel's arms over Grimm's castle as she circled, searching with telescopic vision for a place to release him.

"Where I see fit," said Ariel. "That's where."

"You don't have to be rude," said Wave. "I was just asking."

"On my home planet of Aviana," said Ariel, "any creatures your size can be picked from the floating trees and eaten as a delicacy. I find that I must concentrate on not eating you, and that sometimes makes me grumpy."

"Well," said Wave, "keep up the good work. I want to live."

"I need to find a secluded spot to drop you," Ariel said. "It may take some time...wait, I see it. An abandoned shed alongside the moat about ninety feet below."

Ariel dropped out of the sky against the sun, wings folded back to gain velocity, and Wave screamed again as they shot downward to bank of the moat faster than anyone could see them.

"Ouch!" Wave sat on the ground, rubbing his head. "You dropped me on my head on purpose."

But Ariel was already gone.

Still miffed, Wave got up, ran to the gardener's shed, and hid behind it for a few moments. He looked around in all directions for hostiles before sending a stream of water down from his fingertips directly into the moat.

"This water is practically toxic," he said, upon analysis. "And it's filled with hungry eight-foot-long reptiles with bad dispositions. Romeo, Spirit—are you there?"

"Yes," said Romeo through Spirit's clairvoyant connection. "We're on horseback heading toward the castle. I need you to proceed as planned, Wave. Understood?"

"Time to get naked," he said, and stripped off all his clothes. He stood on the moat's mushy, reed-filled bank and began to dissolve, bleeding into clear fluid until his whole body broke down into tiny liquid molecules that slid into the moat and disappeared under its murky surface.

To the west, crossing the desert, were Romeo and Spirit, who were racing on horseback to reach the Grimm's castle in time.

"The horses are too slow," said Romeo. "We need to be there *now*."

"I can help," said Spirit, who actually floated above her horse's saddle.

"Whatever you do, Spirit," said Romeo. "It's gotta be big."

"Hang on." Spirit paused for a moment and conjured. "*Zin bodwin, eiger ness*."

Within a few seconds, their horses began to neigh and snort roughly and then broke into a hyper-gallop across the desert sands, over the tall iron mountains, and into the valley of the dead to the land of the merciless maniac Peter the Grimm. At this speed, they would arrive in a quarter of the time.

Along the way, Romeo spotted a flaming arrow in the sky, an indication that the queen's young army, commanded by Regent Oman, was in place to block Grimm's retreat if he tried to escape.

"*Ness bodwin, eiger zin*," Spirit conjured again, and on Romeo's command, a visual illusion of a thirty-foot-tall rose spiraled in the sky, large enough to be seen many miles away—a signal to Oman that the rescue plan was underway.

Arriving at Grimm's castle before sunset, Romeo saw that the drawbridge leading into the castle's courtyard was still up, allowing no one to enter or leave. They left their horses tied by the stables and walked the short distance back to the moat.

"Wave?" called Romeo through Spirit, "are you in there?"

"Yes," Wave said, "and it's disgusting."

"The drawbridge is still up," said Romeo. "What happened?"

"Something magic is blocking all the open pipes and ducts around the castle," said Wave. "I can't get in."

"The evil presence I mentioned," said Spirit. "It protects Grimm."

"I'm not afraid," said Romeo. "Wave, if you're up to it, I think this situation calls for a *lift*."

"I can do it," Wave said. "How big?"

"Big enough to break down the door," said Romeo. "For the sake of the queen, we have no time to waste."

A moment later, Wave surfaced at the top of the rolling black water and lifted his arms slowly skyward. Romeo and Spirit stepped back, and people began to gather to watch what they could hardly believe—the moat water was rising up out of its bed, lifting itself higher and higher into the air until the moat's floor could be seen underneath. Wave lifted his arms even higher, and the water obeyed, rising up in the air, the large killer-reptile creatures held inside it. Directed by Wave, the watery mass smashed into the drawbridge with such force that it broke through and poured its contents—brackish water and the agitated, giant, hungry reptiles—inside the castle walls.

"Your friends are outside trying to rescue you, dear Cousin," said Grimm. "But I don't want you to leave. No, we have many things to do together, including starting a family to carry on my lineage."

"You truly are mad, Peter," said Queen Niz, chained to a wall, "if you think I'd have your child. I'd kill myself first."

Grimm got up from his throne and walked slowly past the hanging victims chained to the wall.

"After I tire of torturing you, Cousin," he said, "I'm going to turn you over to my Dark Brigade guards to be used for their pleasure...until it's my turn. Then the sick fun will *really* begin."

The forceful impact of Wave's wall of dirty, giant-reptile-filled moat water that he'd lifted almost thirty feet crashed through the drawbridge and filled the castle's inner courtyard with almost ten feet of water that drowned at least twenty Dark Brigade guards caught in its swirling wake before it washed away.

"Wave," said Spirit. "For someone so small, he is very strong."

"And young," said Romeo. "Compared to our ages, he's but a child."

The water's impact deposited a large number of flapping fish and their predators, the giant, scaly, gray-green-skinned, eight-foot reptile creatures that walked on all fours and had long, snapping jaws, ripping sharp claws to attack anything that moved, and beady little eyes that moved continuously, looking for prey.

"Run!" screamed a guard who had survived the drowning. He tried to make his way to the castle, but he got only about twenty feet when two large creatures jumped in front of him and knocked him down with their tails. Each then grabbed one end of his body in its jaws, and they ripped him in two.

Another thirty guards were torn to pieces by the menacing reptiles and then slowly devoured, some of them while still alive. Smelling more food, some of the large creatures broke their way through the castle's maze of hallways and rooms that led to the centermost point: the torture chamber Grimm had built in a tower as his personal playroom.

Outside the castle walls, Romeo drew his sword from its scabbard.

"Spirit?" asked Romeo. "We need to get in there."

"Zin ness, eiger bodwin," chanted Spirit, and they floated across the moat and entered the castle's unprotected courtyard. The waters had now receded back into the moat, leaving bloated bodies and several large feeding reptiles behind. As the Protectors passed, a giant reptile turned from its human meal and charged Romeo, who backflipped out of the way. On the creature's next run, he was able to eviscerate it with his sharpened sword blade, spilling the creature's guts—including the stomach, which overflowed its contents of human body parts over the courtyard's stones. Thinking himself safe, Romeo lowered his sword when suddenly, another snapping gray-green monster attacked him from behind.

"Ness bodwin, eiger zin," called Spirit, who floated through the creature, blocked its path with magic, and then transmuted it into the castle's water-refilled moat in a cloud of smoke.

"Thanks," Romeo said with a smile. "You saved my life."

Spirit pretended not to notice her attraction to him. "Everyone falls in love with Romeo," she told herself, not quite sure what she wanted.

"Now that I'm inside the castle walls," said Spirit, "I can feel the presence of the queen. She is in that tall tower beyond the main part of the castle. But first we have to pass over this courtyard ahead."

"Then let's go," said Romeo, moving forward.

"Wait!" warned Spirit. She stopped floating, sensing a trap.

"Spirit? What is it?"

"They are very close—the Dark Brigade," she said. "To the left, and behind the stone wall."

Out of the shadows, the Dark Brigade guard, specially trained and uniformed, attacked with their sharp swords drawn—a least a platoon of savagely trained soldiers in heavy body armor wearing pointed metal hats and black masks. Their eyes were dull and lifeless, colored red like blood, as if they were under some sort of magic spell, perhaps for obedience, and could not rebel. The guard marched into the courtyard and lined up along its outer rim, surrounding the two Protectors and practically boxing them in.

"Hah!" yelled Peter the Grimm from the top of the tower roof. He held the bloodied, semiconscious Queen Niz in his arms. "Fools! The two of you cannot pass my Dark Brigade."

"We're trapped," said Romeo. "Any suggestions?"

"Try communicating with Grimm," said Spirit. "Meanwhile, I'll do a magic analysis on the queen's health."

"Release the queen," yelled Romeo, "and we will not hurt you. But if you do not, Grimm, I promise that you will die."

"My cousin is here to stay," said Grimm. "She and I plan to be together forever...or as long as she lives."

"The queen is in very bad shape," said Spirit. "We need to hurry and rescue her."

"Can't you do something from down here?" asked Romeo.

"She's too far away for my healing powers to reach her," Spirit said.

"Then there's only one thing to do," said Romeo. "Charge on."

Burble, gurgle.

A large puddle of liquid that had formed from the remnants of the moat water began to bubble and roll, finally forming itself into the figure of Wave.

"Wave!" said Romeo. "Where have you been?"

"Perfect timing, though," said Spirit.

Wave stepped forward, shaking the water out of one ear.

"I've traveled through the tower's cracks and crevices," Wave said. "I think I know of a way to get us in and take us directly to the queen."

"Let's move."

As the Protectors pressed forward, the Dark Brigade guards did as well, stepping out of their lines all at once toward the three.

"*Zin zin, ness bodwin*," chanted Spirit, and the approaching guards fell into quicksand up to their shoulders. They could not get out. From a different direction, a group of guards rushed forward and encircled Romeo, engaging the master swordsman all at once. The sound of sharpened steel swords smashing and clashing against each other was loud and volatile, but Romeo stood his ground, and he moved like the wind.

Spirit, floating toward him to help, froze when she felt a deep chill. She turned around slowly to confront a nine-foot-tall lizard-skinned monster that stood on two tree-trunk legs and had a double-horned head and a hungry look in its eyes.

"Zin eiger ne—"

She tried to finish her spell but could not, because the monster had grabbed her with one hand and covered her mouth with the other. Spirit turned her body into smoke, slipped out of the monster's arms, and returned to form.

"Ness," she chanted, now able to finish speaking the suffocation spell.

The monster's scaly skin began to move on its own, literally trying to pull away from the creature's body. With a final contortion, the facial skin wrapped, twisted, and covered the creature's mouth and nose, cutting off its air as it struggled fruitlessly to pull its own skin off. Within a minute, the creature fell over, head first to the ground.

Romeo used his skill, speed, and courage to defeat all the Dark Brigade guards who had set upon him at the same time. As their bodies fell, Wave pulled moisture from two passing clouds and used it to flush them down the drain.

"Did we get all of them?" asked Romeo, breathing heavily. Sweat showed through his blousy shirt, exposing a lean, tight, near-perfect body underneath.

"Not quite all of them," said Peter the Grimm from the roof.

Another platoon of Dark Brigade guards poured in from the rear corridor, their spears pointed straight ahead.

"You'll never defeat me!" cried Grimm. He laughed and left the roof, still holding the dazed queen.

"We're going in to rescue the queen," said Romeo over Spirit's clairvoyant link. "Ariel, clean up here."

Out of the blue, Arial, wings pinned back for speed and swinging her mighty sword, dived down to the courtyard and at the last minute pulled up enough to cut down the guards one after the other until they were all dead. Then she headed back to where she always felt most comforted—away from humans, out in the open sky.

Romeo, Spirit, and Wave ran into the castle, fighting a few stray guards or slimy snake-skinned creatures that remained to prowl the hallways. They headed toward a winding staircase that disappeared into the ceiling, leading to the tall tower Grimm used to hold and torture his victims. Once up the staircase and into the tower, the Protectors encountered row after row of human skulls and bones lined up in patterns along the walls, some painted in bright colors, and others dripping with fresh red blood. At the top of the stairs, they stepped out and saw a small wooden door, brown against the gray walls. As they approached, the stench of rotting corpses and spilled blood stopped them cold.

"This man is very sick," Wave said as he stood before the door. "I'm actually scared."

"We need to be careful," said Romeo. "But to stop him, we need to go in strong—even if it jeopardizes the queen's safety."

"It won't," said Spirit. "I'll see to that."

"Very well," said Romeo. "Wave?"

Wave molded himself into a battering ram of water and broke down the door. The Protectors rushed into the room.

"Come in," said Peter the Grimm. He sat calmly on his wooden throne, holding a sword in his hand. "We've been expecting you."

All around them hung the bodies of the living dead, some mutilated so badly they were unrecognizable. Hanging behind Grimm's throne was Queen Niz.

"Majesty," Romeo called out. "Are you all right?"

She did not answer.

"You there," said Grimm, pointing to Wave. "You drowned a lot of my guards with your moisture. Maybe it's time you dried out."

The floor underneath Wave burst into flames, some rising six feet tall, surrounding him, and the heat caused him to slowly evaporate. Romeo rushed over to help but could not break through the wall of flames.

"And for you, my ethereal beauty," Grimm said to Spirit. "For you, I have the wind to blow you away."

Into the room spun a whirling dervish that trapped Spirit's essence in its tornadic winds. It held her securely but did not extinguish the fires surrounding Wave.

"Wave!" shouted Romeo. "Try to go *under* the flames. Spirit, I—"

Grimm got up from his throne and moved toward Romeo, his gleaming sword drawn. When he was close enough, Romeo leaped forward with his sword and began to fight, Grimm jumping from one part of the room to the other, pursued by Romeo as their silver swords clashed.

"You are a good swordsman, Romeo," said Grimm. "But I've trained with the best. You are no match for my skills."

To prove it, Grimm slashed Romeo's white shirt to pieces and in two precise movements cut an *X* into his skin.

"Ah," said Romeo. "I see you like the sight of blood, madman. Wait until you see your own!"

With a mighty lunge, Romeo cut Grimm's hand, and he dropped his sword. As Romeo moved in to stab him, a slimy creature from the moat, perhaps a lost, hungry juvenile, entered the room and jumped into the middle of the sword fight. Distracted, Romeo cut its throat, unaware Grimm had retrieved his sword until its blade pierced the left side of his back from behind.

"My cousin is mine," said Grimm. "You'll not take her from me."

In the center of the flames, Wave struggled to find a way out, but the floor would not budge, even when he tried to punch his way through. Spirit was not faring any better. Her ethereal body was still trapped in the dervish's whirlwind, spinning around and around, unable to concentrate on a rescue spell to free herself from its clutches.

"You're beaten, Grimm!" said Romeo. "Give up."

"Look who's beaten, Romeo," said Grimm. "You're the one bleeding, and your teammates are no help at all. I've got you where I want you, fool—right here in my tower, where I rule, not the Protectors."

The seriously wounded and disarmed, Romeo was about to fall when Ariel swooped in silently, crashed through the tower roof and grabbed Grimm by his shoulder blades with her sharp talons, forcing him to drop his sword. She lifted him up into the air, flying through the hole she'd made upon entering. Ariel flew miles away to the side of a mountain cliff, where she dragged the shocked Grimm, kicking and screaming, into a cave, cut off his head with her sword, ripped open his chest, and ate his still-beating heart.

Back in the tower, the flames died out around Wave, and the dervish disappeared, releasing Spirit. They rushed to Romeo's side.

"Are you all right?" asked Spirit, concerned.

"Let me," said Wave. He washed away the blood from Romeo's wounds and stepped back in surprise. "But your cuts—they're healed!"

"Wasn't me," said Spirit.

"My body heals itself," said Romeo. "Being immortal and all."

"Well," said Wave, sitting on the floor. "That certainly didn't go well."

"What?" Romeo asked.

"Our mission," said Wave. "We almost blew it, and Grimm was about to…"

"Ariel got him, Wave," said Romeo. "It's called teamwork."

Spirit floated over to Queen Niz, who still hung in chains.

"Your Highness," she said, bowing. "Let me help you."

Spirit reached out her hand and grabbed the queen's. Almost immediately, the queen began to mumble and move, opening her eyes and trying to grasp her situation.

"Where?" she asked.

"You're safe now," Romeo said.

Wave pulled the queen's chains out of the wall, freeing her, while

Spirit worked on getting her mobile. Then with the queen stabilized, Wave and Romeo went around freeing the others in the room. Spirit healing them as best she could. Finally, they all walked away from that wretched place.

A few days later, Queen Niz wanted to give thanks to the Protectors for saving her life and defeating her evil cousin, Peter the Grimm. She gave a huge celebration in her castle to thank them and to welcome back the good people who had fled under the evil Grimm's regime. The celebration was a big success, and Romeo seemed quite taken with the queen. At one point, he kissed her hand as they danced together. Near the end of the celebration, Oman, father of the queen, stood up to toast the Protectors.

"My dear Protectors," Oman began, raising his golden goblet. "We owe you such a great debt of gratitude for returning to us our beloved Queen Niz and removing that evil stain on humanity called Grimm—a monster, really, who'd hurt so many lives. To these Protectors I offer the keys to the kingdom and a welcome anywhere you go...with one exception. Romeo, I heard about your reputation with women, so if you tempt my pretty young daughter with your manly charms, you'll have to marry her, too. Cheers."

"Father!" said Queen Niz, exasperated.

"It would be my honor to marry your daughter, Oman," said Romeo. "If she'd have me?"

"I do," said Queen Niz, and everyone rejoiced—except the heart-broken Spirit, who faded through the castle's walls, going on her way alone. She never spoke of Romeo again.

THE END

ABOUT THE AUTHOR

Nate Stack, writer and visual artist, lives in the United States. In addition to the Silver Age series of books, which includes *Chiara X*, *Ghost Town*, and *Lady Vampyr*, Stack has written several plays, including, *Gitmo Serenade, Beach Ball, After, The Prisoner's Wife, Three Women,* and *The Men's Room.*

Made in the USA
San Bernardino, CA
20 December 2018